Maple's Theory of FUN

Kate McMillan & Ruthie Prillaman

ALADDIN
NEW YORK · LONDON · TORONTO · SYDNEY · NEW DELHI

🪔 ALADDIN

An imprint of Simon & Schuster Children's Publishing Division
1230 Avenue of the Americas, New York, New York 10020
First Aladdin hardcover edition March 2024
Copyright © 2024 by Ruthie Prillaman and Kate McMillan
All rights reserved, including the right of reproduction in whole or in part in any form.
ALADDIN and related logo are registered trademarks of Simon & Schuster, LLC.
Simon & Schuster: Celebrating 100 Years of Publishing in 2024
For information about special discounts for bulk purchases, please contact
Simon & Schuster Special Sales at 1-866-506-1949 or business@simonandschuster.com.
The Simon & Schuster Speakers Bureau can bring authors to your live event.
For more information or to book an event contact the Simon & Schuster
Speakers Bureau at 1-866-248-3049 or visit our website at www.simonspeakers.com.
Designed by Tiara Iandiorio
The illustrations for this book were rendered digitally.
The text of this book was set in Kabouter.
Manufactured in the United States of America 0124 BVG
10 9 8 7 6 5 4 3 2 1
Library of Congress Cataloging-in-Publication Data
Names: McMillan, Kate, author. | Prillaman, Ruthie, author.
Title: Maple's theory of fun / by Kate McMillan and Ruthie Prillaman.
Description: First Aladdin hardcover edition. | New York : Aladdin, 2024. |
Summary: To get her best friend back, anxious and inventive eleven-year-old Maple performs a scientific experiment to uncover the secret to becoming fun.
Identifiers: LCCN 2023008877 (print) | LCCN 2023008878 (ebook) |
ISBN 9781665941037 (hc) | ISBN 9781665941044 (ebook)
Subjects: CYAC: Anxiety–Fiction. | Science–Experiments–Fiction. | Best friends–Fiction. | Friendship–Fiction. | Diaries–Fiction. | LCGFT: Diary fiction. | Novels.
Classification: LCC PZ7.M4787823 Map 2024 (print) | LCC PZ7.M4787823 (ebook) | DDC [Fic]–dc23
LC record available at https://lccn.loc.gov/2023008877
LC ebook record available at https://lccn.loc.gov/2023008878

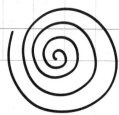

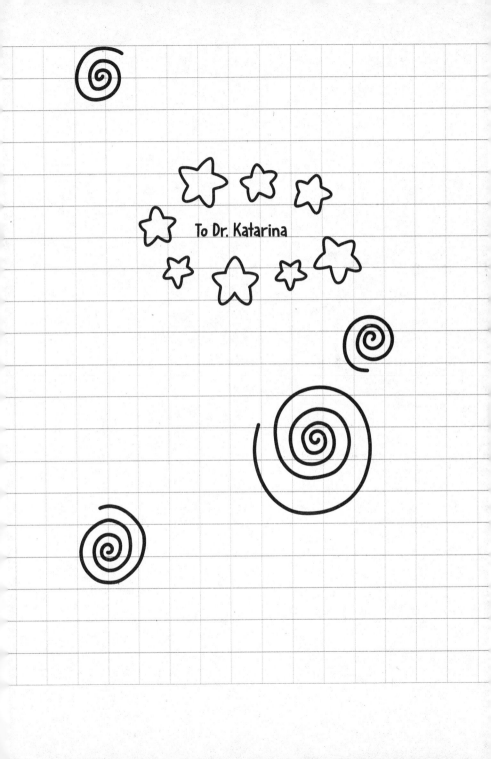

To Dr. Katarina

Space Center Houston: front lawn.

There's a 99% chance that today will be the BEST day of my life.

In T-minus 62 minutes, my best friend, Sunny, and I will be shaking hands with a real NASA astronaut. And not just any astronaut but objectively the coolest, smartest, most competent astronaut who has ever existed on Earth (I can't speak for undiscovered exoplanets):

Jackie Grand.

Jackie

Me passing the wrench carefully so it doesn't float away into deep space.

1

Inspiring and informative fact #1: Jackie Grand has piloted 11 space flights, completed 7 space walks, and collected over ONE THOUSAND intergalactic dust particles.

She's signing autographs at the NASA Fun Fair for a whole 45 MINUTES, even though she definitely has a jam-packed training schedule before her next mission.

Inspiring and informative fact #2: Jackie Grand 3D-printed the first pizza in space. Flavor: cheese.

I know that if I don't have an airtight plan, I'm going to say something stupid in front of Jackie, or worse, freeze up and say nothing at all like I ~~sometimes~~ often do. Fortunately, Sunny and I came up with Operation Airtight Plan, which is just our way of saying we wrote a speech in advance. Well, I guess I wrote all of it, but the point is, we're going to say it together.

OPERATION AIRTIGHT PLAN

(DO NOT THROW AWAY)

<u>Sunny</u>: Greetings, Jackie Grand. (Shake hand.) My name is Sunny Gwon, and this is my best friend and scientific collaborator:

Maple: Maple McNutt.

<u>Sunny</u>: It is an honor and a privilege to stand in your presence. Maple wants you to know that you are pretty much the entire reason that she wants to be an astronaut when she grows up. And why she has attempted multiple times to make a pizza on her dad's 3D printer.

Maple: It's true.

<u>Sunny</u>: Maple also wants you to know that she watched your ScienceRocksRadio interview on YouTube, and it inspired her to request a journal EXACTLY like yours for Christmas, which she received.

<u>Sunny</u> (continued): It even has graph paper like yours, which is essential for recording FACTS.

Maple: And drawing ACCURATE diagrams.

<u>Sunny</u>: I would be honored if you would give me a high five so that I may high-five a hand that has gone to space.

Maple: Whereas I would be honored if you would please sign your autograph right <u>here</u> very neatly.

<u>Sunny</u> and Maple: Thank you. (Hand over journal.)

Jackie Grand _____

I feel way better about the speech since Sunny's doing it with me. He should be here any minute.

I texted Sunny (actually his dad because Sunny doesn't have a cell phone yet):

> T-minus 50 minutes until JACKIE GRAND! — Me

> are you at NASTY yet?

> *I mean NASTY

> *NASA

Mr. Gwon: cominnggggg! be there in literally ONE SECOND

hehehe nasty

One ... two ... three ... maybe he meant one MINUTE away.

5:43 p.m.

Now it's been exactly THREE minutes. I'm starting to wonder if something happened. Maybe they got a flat tire?

5

5:44 p.m.

Or maybe they parked next to the roller coaster the exact second it derailed and the roller coaster car smashed into Mr. Gwon's sunroof? I'm looking up whether that's even possible.

5:46 p.m.

Okay, according to an <u>extremely legitimate website</u> <u>SPECIALIZING</u> in theme-park disasters, it's not very likely. But not impossible.

5:47 p.m.

My mom asked why I'm sitting by myself, "doodling," instead of being first in line to meet Jackie. She pointed out that some of my other friends, like Mahogany Perez and Ovi Nagar, are already lining up. I told her, yet AGAIN, that I have to wait for Sunny to execute Operation Airtight Plan, which won't be so airtight if he did in fact get smooshed by a derailed roller coaster.

6

Also, I'm not "doodling." I'm drawing accurate diagrams.

5:50 p.m.

My mom keeps looking over my shoulder at my phone.

What are you looking at?

Nothing, just roller coaster crash statistics.

Maple, you have to stop googling everything. It just makes you worry for no reason.

Your sister went on the roller coaster, and she's fine!

How do you know she didn't rupture a brain cell . . . her ONLY brain cell?

Why don't you put down the phone and decorate a rocket with me!

glitter

even MORE glitter

7

I should mention that my mom works in the NASA PR department, planning educational events for Rocket Grrls, a club that's supposed to "get girls excited about science." My mom set up this paint-your-own-rocket booth because she FALSELY believes that girls won't be interested in space exploration unless she slathers every rocket in pink sparkly paint.

I told her for approximately the twelfth time that sparkles would be disastrous in zero gravity because debris as small as one millimeter can severely disable subsystems on board a spacecraft. She said I need to "take a deep breath and have fun."

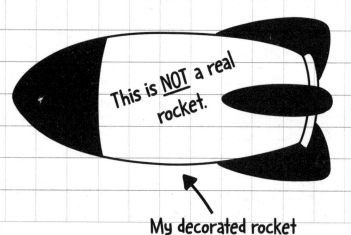

This is NOT a real rocket.

My decorated rocket

You know what? I'm not going to let it bother me. Not on the best day of my entire life. I wonder if Jackie Grand has entered the premises.

I'm also wondering if Sunny's alive.

5:57 p.m.

> **are you alive?** — Me

Mr. Gwon: 👍 sorrryyyyyyyy

carpooling with Jared n we stopped for smoothies 🥤🥤🥤

C U SOOOOOOONNN

Ugh. Jared again.

Every day is magical

when YOU are the magic.

NOTE: I specifically told my parents that I wanted the scientific notebook with graph paper only, NOT with inspirational quotes.

9

Sunny and I started sixth grade this year at a new middle school that has a special science program. I was kind of nervous about meeting a bunch of new kids that I didn't know from elementary school or preschool or NASA day care (where Sunny and I met as babies). Fortunately, most of the other kids are really nice and/or smart.

NAME	SMART?	NICE?
Mahogany Perez	✓	✓
Ovi Nagar		✓

Unfortunately, there's also Jared Grody.

NAME	SMART?	NICE?
Jared Grody	NEITHER	

I really wish Sunny wouldn't carpool with Jared. Jared has NO RESPECT for getting places on time, or for anything, really. He's in computer science with us, and all he does is draw butts in DigiPaint. Jared even got Sunny to participate in the butt painting, which caused Sunny to get his first B+. Mr. Gwon and I were not pleased.

Moment from 1.5 months ago:

6:06 p.m.

11

6:10 p.m.

Eat me!

Yo. yo. yo!

Save us!

Sunny was supposed to draw in this box.

6:13 p.m.

We're in line! Sunny and I are going to run the speech one to three more times. Jared went off to ride the roller coaster, thankfully. . . . Maybe it will get stuck upside down for the rest of the night. Or, no, I take that back—I don't want the blood to sink to his brain and his head to explode. Taking it back!!

Despite my facts about the dangers of glitter, my mom still let Sunny take a whole bottle from the paint-

12

your-own-rocket booth so we could "sparkle up the evening!" I think my mom is a bad influence on Sunny.

Sunny just poured glitter in my hair.

No I didn't!

Yes, he did. I'm no longer
permitting Sunny to record
mistruths in this journal.

I can't let Jackie see me like this, even if Sunny says
I look "mega-fancy" with glitter hair. Picking out each
glitter particle as we speak.

Operation Airtight Plan is ready to go. I'm only about 36%

nervous now that Sunny's here. I hope I make a good impression on Jackie so that when we one day become colleagues in space (hopefully), she'll remember me fondly.

6:22 p.m.

Ugh, Jared just showed up in line. I guess the roller coaster didn't get stuck. He said he saw a girl further up with the longest ponytail he'd ever seen. Specifically "one billion feet long," which is highly unlikely, given that the world record is 18 feet. (I looked it up.) Jared clearly doesn't believe in FACTS.

Jared tried to convince Sunny to get out of line and go get dino nuggets instead of waiting and waiting to meet "some lady." ... SOME LADY???

Inspiring and informative fact #3: Jackie Grand went to the Olympics for jujitsu and came in fourth place. Which means she could 100% kick Jared's butt extremely hard if she wanted to. (Which she wouldn't. She obeys laws.)

I almost told Jared that, but then Sunny stepped in.

I just have to do this random thing really quickly with Maple. I'll come meet you after!

Face = 42% red

One of the WORST things about Jared is that he makes Sunny act all weird and say stuff that I don't think he really means. For example, why would Sunny call meeting the most important person in the world "this random thing," and why would he want the best moment of our lives to be over really quickly?

I probably should be more careful about who sees my journal now that I've written all this sensitive material. Changing my journal status to HIGHLY classified.

6:26 p.m.

Jared asked why I was doodling so much in my coloring book instead of "living in the moment." But before I could correct him, he wandered off.

6:27 p.m.

I just saw Ponytail Girl up ahead of us with my own eyes, and I can confirm that the ponytail is in fact very long. Although not "one billion feet" like Jared falsely claimed. Sunny dared me to touch it, but I said no, so he dared himself to touch it. Right before he made contact, the girl turned around and said, "If you touch my ponytail, it will eat you." We couldn't tell if she was kidding, so Sunny didn't do it.

Approximately 4.123 feet

6:30 p.m.

I'm probably 48% nervous now. Apparently, Jackie's gravitational simulation practice is running overtime so there's a five-minute delay. I hope I don't forget the speech and say something embarrassing.

6:32 p.m.

I wonder if I should tell Jackie about the birthday cake I had two years ago with her face on it. Is that weird?

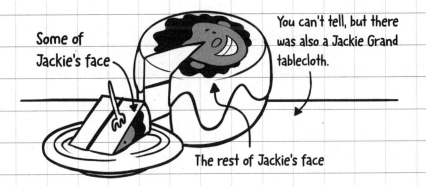

Some of Jackie's face

You can't tell, but there was also a Jackie Grand tablecloth.

The rest of Jackie's face

6:33 p.m.

Sunny says it's probably weird. I'm going to play it safe and stick to our script.

6:34 p.m.

They said it's going to be more like ten minutes.

6:35 p.m.

SO EXCITED. CAN'T WAIT.

6:36 p.m.

SO EXCITED x 100!

6:38 p.m.

Sunny said maybe I should put my journal away so we can "live in the moment" like Jared said. Even though I do not respect Jared's opinion at all, I guess I should be FULLY PRESENT when I meet Jackie. Old Maple signing off. Get ready for Maple 2.0!

Shoot for the moon.
You'll land in the stars.

FALSE. You will only have enough fuel to get to the moon and NO FURTHER.

18

Maple 1.0 here.

I know I said there was a 99% chance that today would be the best day of my life. I guess that also meant that there was a 1% chance that today would be the WORST day of my life.

We were standing in line to meet Jackie Grand when Sunny got a text from Jared on his dad's phone. (I thought I was the only person allowed to text his dad's phone?) From what I could see, Jared's text said something like:

Jared BRUHHHHHH

COME CHCK OUT DA BOUNCY HOUZZ OBSTACLE COURSSSE THINGGGG NOWW!!!!"

Jared insisted that the line for the bouncy house was "real short" and the obstacle course "doesn't even look hard" and "they're closing really soon so stop being a poop in the boring line and COME ON."

Jackie's running super late anyway. We can do it reaallllyyyyy quickly!

I don't really do rides.

It's an EXPERIENCE, not a ride!!

Then Sunny said "pleeeasssse" in at least four languages (English, Korean, Spanish, and binary). He even did the puppy-dog eyes, which made it really hard to say no.

Since they told us Jackie was still changing out of her space suit, I figured we had at least fifteen minutes until she got there, and the line behind us wasn't that long. So I said, "Fine, I guess," in English only.

20

We went over to the bouncy-house obstacle course, and SURPRISE! Jared had misrepresented not one but two aspects of the "experience." (1) The line was extremely long, and (2) the obstacle course looked EXTREMELY treacherous.

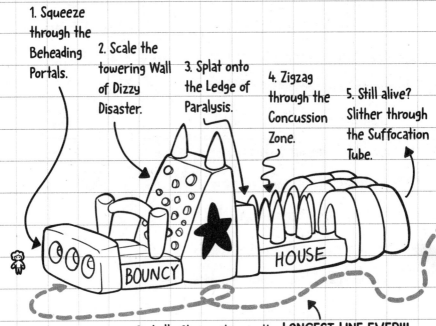

1. Squeeze through the Beheading Portals.

2. Scale the towering Wall of Dizzy Disaster.

3. Splat onto the Ledge of Paralysis.

4. Zigzag through the Concussion Zone.

5. Still alive? Slither through the Suffocation Tube.

BOUNCY

HOUSE

And all after waiting in the LONGEST LINE EVER!!!

While we waited in line, I did some emergency research about bouncy houses on my phone. Did you know:

1. It's not unheard of for bouncy houses to pop.

2. The average bouncy house gets cleaned ONLY ONCE every three years.

3. Bouncy houses were the cause of 300 injuries and 11 deaths last year. (Source: Bounce House Horror Stories)

Jared thought all that was HILARIOUS. What is hilarious about injury and death?!?! Sunny was also laughing, which was completely out of character since I know for a FACT that he bawled when his fish got squished in the tank filter and died last year. I don't know why Sunny thinks he has to go along with everything Jared says.

The line was moving extremely slowly, so I pointed out to Sunny that we might be cutting it close to do Operation Airtight Plan, a.k.a. say our speech to Jackie.

Why do you need Sunny with you to say hi to someone? Is he your babysitter?

Face = 53% red

I'm noooooooottttttttttttt!

Sunny pulled me aside and assured me that the line moved wayyyy faster than it seemed because they took three people at once, but if I was really nervous about the time, I could go do the speech without him and he wouldn't be mad. I didn't really know what to say because that would defeat the WHOLE point of Operation Airtight Plan. So I decided to wait it out with Sunny.

But then one kid had an accident on the rock wall, so they spent a whole five minutes sanitizing it with wet wipes. Don't people know that those only kill 99% of germs? What about the remaining 1%? What about the SCENT PARTICLES? I tried to distract myself by rereading the Bounce House Horror Stories death statistics.

Jared and Sunny came up with a strategy for how to execute the "sickest triple bounce of all time," although I was very distracted by my research. It started to feel like there was something squishing my lungs, and barely ANY air was going in. Then my fingers started to tingle. Then my whole body went numb. When we finally reached the front, I couldn't take even one step closer to the obstacle course. At first I thought maybe I was panicking, but then I remembered this bone-fusing disease I'd seen on the internet called ankylosing spondylitis and felt pretty sure that I had that. My pediatrician has told me on multiple occasions that I don't have ankylosing spondylitis, but seeing as I was COMPLETELY frozen in place, I'm not convinced.

My face must have looked even paler than usual, because the bouncy-house guard offered me some of his PERSONAL water bottle. (Which I refused. That's gross.)

24

What Is Ankylosing Spondylitis?

- general discomfort ☑
- joint pain (maybe a little?)
  some
- ~~whole~~ body inflammation ☑
- very rare: total paralysis ←
  not yet but probably soon

Occurs in less than 1% of the US population, typically among men older than 17 **but still!**

I could tell that Sunny really wanted me to participate in the triple bounce because he pointed out that "even four-year-olds are getting on the ride—I mean EXPERIENCE!" I tried to clarify that four-year-olds don't have fully developed brains, but Jared interrupted as usual:

Bro, are we doing this, or do I need to find some randos who aren't scared?

I'M not scared. MAPLE'S the one who's scared!

Face = 76% red

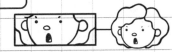

25

I wanted to remind them that THEY were the ones who'd LIED about the difficulty level of the obstacle course, and never did I sign a contract to plummet to my DEATH. The words weren't coming out of my mouth, though, so all I said was "I can't do it" really quietly.

I guess Jared didn't hear me, because he elbowed Sunny and said, "Whatever, babysitter," and started laughing, which made Sunny shoot up to 99% red (the reddest I have ever seen him). I think Sunny kind of snapped right then, because he looked me right in the face and shouted:

You ALWAYS do this, Maple! Why can't you just be FUN?!

The bouncy-house guard interrupted before I could get my voice box working again and told us to go ahead, but since I was paralyzed in place, I obviously couldn't go anywhere. Jared and Sunny went with the random four-year-old in line behind us, who probably already had ten broken bones from the triple bounce. I didn't know what else to do except wait until the numbness went away, which took forever. At least twenty-one kids went on the bouncy house before I could move my ankles at all. When I finally recovered, I hurried back to the line for Jackie Grand, but by the time I got there, the booth was empty and the line was gone.

I missed it.

I guess I lost track of time while I was waiting for my ankylosing spondylitis to go away. I ran around the entire perimeter of the Fun Fair, and I even checked in all the bathrooms (they really should have hand sanitizer in there), but Jackie Grand was definitely gone.

That was probably the only chance I'll ever get to meet Jackie. I can't believe I missed it. I can't believe I RUINED it.

I barely saw Sunny for the rest of the night, and for all I know, he died in the Suffocation Tube and nobody bothered to call his emergency contact (me).

I'm hiding in the car right now to avoid rocket-booth cleanup duty with my mom. Since my dad is traveling for work, my sister and I are her only source of unpaid labor. I'm not exactly in the mood.

I keep thinking about what Sunny said in the bouncy-house line.

~~Why does he think~~
~~Why can't I just~~

What did Sunny mean when he said I "always" do this?

Maybe he's referring to the time I had to go home early from his laser-tag birthday because of a flash-flood warning? Would that count? Or the time I made him throw out a whole box of Fruit Roll-Ups because the expiration date was within two days and I didn't want him to get toxic-mold poisoning?

My mom just got back to the car with about 30 sparkly rockets and the unshowered cavewoman who lives with us, a.k.a. my older sister, Juniper, a.k.a. my second-least-favorite person after Jared. My mom looked at me VERY judgmentally and said that her rocket booth was an absolute hit, aside from when I almost spoiled the fun with my explosion statistics. Juniper said that "everybody always has fun when Maple leaves," and now my mom is yelling at her for making fun of me.

Why does everyone keep saying the F word?

FUN.

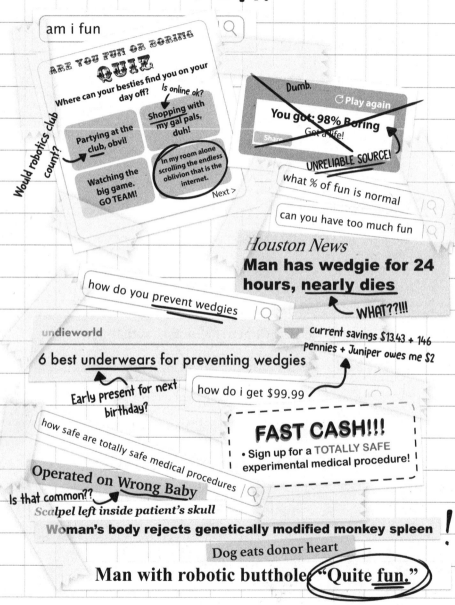

am i fun

ARE YOU FUN OR BORING QUIZ

Where can your besties find you on your day off?

Is online ok?

Partying at the club, obvi!

Shopping with my gal pals, duh!

Watching the big game. GO TEAM!

In my room alone scrolling the endless oblivion that is the internet.

Next >

Would robotics club count??

Dumb.

↻ Play again

You got: 98% Boring

Get a life!

Share

UNRELIABLE SOURCE!

what % of fun is normal

can you have too much fun

Houston News

Man has wedgie for 24 hours, nearly dies

WHAT??!!!

how do you prevent wedgies

undieworld

current savings $13.43 + 146 pennies + Juniper owes me $2

6 best underwears for preventing wedgies

Early present for next birthday?

how do i get $99.99

how safe are totally safe medical procedures

FAST CASH!!!
- Sign up for a TOTALLY SAFE experimental medical procedure!

Operated on Wrong Baby

Is that common??

Scalpel left inside patient's skull

Woman's body rejects genetically modified monkey spleen

Dog eats donor heart

Man with robotic butthole "Quite fun."

Jackie Grand would probably approach this
scientifically.

Testable question: Am I fun?

Real World Data		Fun/Not fun
My mom — You almost ruined the fun!		Not fun
My dad — *Cannot confirm, but I'm sure if he were here, he would agree with Mom.		Not fun
Juniper — Everyone has fun when Maple leaves.		Not fun
Jared — yawn		Not fun
Sunny — You ALWAYS do this, Maple. Why can't you just BE FUN?		Not fun

Fun: 0. Not fun: ℍℍ.

Conclusion: **I AM NOT FUN.**

NO!

*A positive attitude
is all you need.*

It's been approximately 36 hours since the (un)Fun Fair. I'm not exactly sure whether Sunny and I are supposed to sit together in science like normal, or if it's going to be weird.

8:12 a.m.

Update: It's weird.

When I got to class, Jared's friend Titus Jemison was sitting in my usual seat next to Sunny. I tried to wave, but Sunny didn't even look up.

Scent particles

Sunny

Titus

8:15 a.m.

Do you think Sunny specifically ASKED Titus to sit there, or did Titus just sit down without even giving Sunny the chance to fight for my seat?

8:16 a.m.

Do you think Titus Jemison is fun?

8:17 a.m.

I guess the only good thing about sitting next to the trash can is that there's an empty seat right behind me. That means nobody can cheat off my tests. OR peek at my journal.

8:19 a.m.

I take it back, the seat is now occupied . . . by the girl from the Fun Fair with the really long ponytail!

Mr. Wormley asked her to "quickly" introduce herself.

Lada

I am Lada Quiche. I just moved here with my mom and my uncles from Hungary. My favorite book is The Apothecary's Daughter series, books 1-17 but not book 4. My favorite food is doboshturtle (?), which is a Hungarian cake with many layers that alternate between cake and cream and caramel and cake.

My favorite dance is rhythmic gymnastics, but I also like ballroom and hip-hop. My favorite material is nylon. And my—

You can stop there, Lada.

Mr. Wormley

I think she would've kept going for a long time, but apparently, we have something REALLY IMPORTANT to go over in class. Mr. Wormley is making us all do a drumroll.

Louder, you guys! LOUDER!!!

He just flipped over the whiteboard to reveal . . .

Oh no.

The Invention Convention is a really big deal. Every year, all the sixth graders compete by coming up with a brand-new invention that will "change the world." The winner gets to have a MINOR PLANET NAMED AFTER THEM.

Sunny and I have been talking about doing the Invention Convention together for at least 3.5 years. We even made a PACT. We even named our planet!

Planet MUNNY

Chocolate lake

Astronaut dogs

There's NO way Sunny would betray a pact.

8:28 a.m.

Mr. Wormley just complimented me on how rigorously
I'm taking notes, so I should probably actually take notes.
Apparently:

1. We have five weeks to learn about inventions
before we have to sign up with our teams.
2. We can work in teams of up to six.
3. Teammates must be fellow sixth graders
as defined by the Timber Cove Middle School
Handbook. **NO PARENTS.**

I glanced over at Sunny, but he didn't notice. It doesn't mean that much, though, because he's all the way across the room and he probably needs glasses anyway.

8:31 a.m.

Just because he didn't sit with me today doesn't mean he would betray the pact. Right?

Inventions Unit: WS #1 (Due Next Monday)

1. Problem in society that needs a solution: Sunny didn't sit with me in science even though we sort of have an unspoken agreement to sit together.

2. Why is this a problem? I'm starting to feel nervous about all our future plans, such as:
   - The Invention Convention
   - 3D-printing more aliens on my dad's 3D printer. And fake pizzas. And egg cups (my idea).
   - Sitting together in computer science
   - The Invention Convention
   - Walking to the bus lane together
   - Going to the Moondog 3 premiere
   - Discovering a new star system

-THE INVENTION CONVENTION

3. How would you solve this problem? ~~~~!?!?

37

I'm picking up a new worksheet from Mr. Wormley at the end of class. . . . I don't think I can turn this one in.

3:20 p.m.

Update: Sunny didn't sit with me in computer science.

4:13 p.m.

Update: I waited by my locker at the end of the day, but Sunny didn't show up.

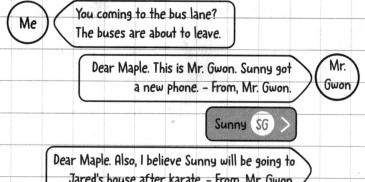

Me: You coming to the bus lane? The buses are about to leave.

Mr. Gwon: Dear Maple. This is Mr. Gwon. Sunny got a new phone. – From, Mr. Gwon.

Sunny SG >

Dear Maple. Also, I believe Sunny will be going to Jared's house after karate. – From, Mr. Gwon.

Me: Oh, okay.

Sunny got a phone?!?!?! I guess I'm not his emergency contact anymore.

I bet he already texted Jared two hundred times even though he swore on his favorite geode that he would text me first. Or maybe it's one of those phones for kids that only has two buttons and you can only call 911 or your parents. Maybe?

I walked to the bus lane by myself. Well, I actually walked with Mahogany Perez, who went on the whole time about how much she likes Lars Ip and maybe he likes her too but maybe not since he didn't hang out with her that much at the Fun Fair. But also where was I at the Fun Fair? And OOOOOH did I want to see the pink glitter-pen autograph she got from Jackie Grand?

The point is that Sunny didn't walk with me.

One day of data is definitely not enough. It could be an outlier, like that one time my foot fell asleep and my pediatrician said it didn't need to be amputated after falling asleep one time.

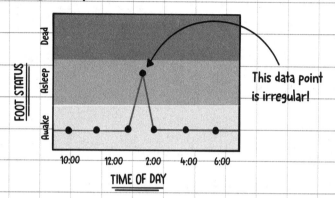

If Sunny sits with me tomorrow, then I'll just stop worrying about everything that happened today. We can still 3D-print stuff and go to the Moondog 3 premiere next month and be best friends like we have been for 7.2 years even if I'm not the most fun person in the world.

He'll probably sit with me tomorrow.

Tuesday, 8:11 a.m.

Update: He didn't sit with me today, either.

Wednesday, 4:14 p.m.

Update: He didn't walk with me to the bus again.

Thursday, 8:11 a.m.

Update: Ughhhhhhh

Friday, 11:16 a.m.

I went to the Maker Lab at lunch to take another crack at that invention worksheet. The Maker Lab is where a bunch of us go every day to conduct important business on the computers (and also eat lunch). Sunny usually sits next to me to play Dinotown AT LEAST two days a week while I work on my computer science homework, although he hasn't come in this week at all.

Where Sunny sometimes sits

Computer with good graphics card

Virtual reality (works sometimes)

Projector screen

Sewing

Electronics station, a.k.a. lost and found

Mahogany Perez was there helping Ovi Nagar with his homework at her usual computer. She asked what I was writing in my journal.

Ooooh, are you planning your invention already? Are you doing it with Sunny? Do you know what you're going to do? Can I see?

No, I'm doing an important math problem.

Important math problem:

What is the probability that Sunny will be my partner for the Invention Convention?

50% he will honor our pact

50% he will betray the pact and find someone else

50% = 1/2 = 0.5

0.5 + 0.5 = 1 ← I'm not sure what that means.

I found the pact that Sunny and I made years ago, stuffed into my bookshelf.

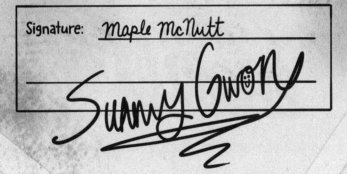

Maple and Sunny's UNBREAKABLE pact

We solemnly swear to be partners for the Invention Convention NO MATTER WHAT. Even if there's a Category 5 hurricane, tsunami, alien invasion, people turn into pizzas, <u>Planet of the Apes</u> happens, or one of us gets ankylosing spondylitis.

Signature: *Maple McNutt*

Sunny Gwon

Is Sunny REALLY going to throw away 7.2 years of friendship and betray AN UNBREAKABLE PACT . . . just because I'm not FUN??

4:53 p.m.

I'm going to try that worksheet one more time.

Inventions Unit: WS #1 (Due Next Monday)

1. Problem in society that needs a solution: I'm not fun.

2. Why is this a problem? If I'm not fun, Sunny might not want to do the Invention Convention with me even though we make the PERFECT team. We invent things together ALL the time! It's pretty much our THING. So if we can't even be partners for that, then what's left of our whole friendship?

3. How would you solve this problem? Become fun?

That's impossible. Fun is something you're born with, like a lot of moles or brown hair. You can't change that.

Well, you CAN get moles surgically removed.

And I guess you CAN dye your hair. My sister, Juniper, dyed her hair Cheeto orange once, and my mom even made her dye it BACK to brown.

What if there's a way to actually BECOME fun? I mean, a scientifically proven way. And if I just follow the right steps, Sunny will think I'm fun enough to be his partner?

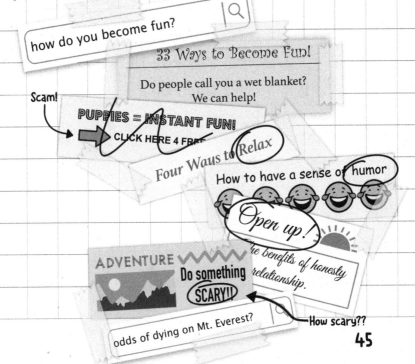

how do you become fun?

33 Ways to Become Fun!

Do people call you a wet blanket?
We can help!

Scam!

PUPPIES = INSTANT FUN!
CLICK HERE 4 FREE

Four Ways to Relax

How to have a sense of humor

Open up!

ADVENTURE
Do something SCARY!!

he benefits of honesty
relationship.

odds of dying on Mt. Everest?

How scary??

45

I HAVE IT.

I consulted 86 different websites and found four requirements that showed up on almost every single list.

MAPLE'S WORKING THEORY OF FUN

To become fun, one must:

1. Relax
2. Have a sense of humor
3. Open up
4. Do something scary

If I can just master these four elements, I. WILL. BECOME. FUN.

I have four weeks to apply my theory if I want to get Sunny back before we sign up for Invention Convention teams. No time to waste.

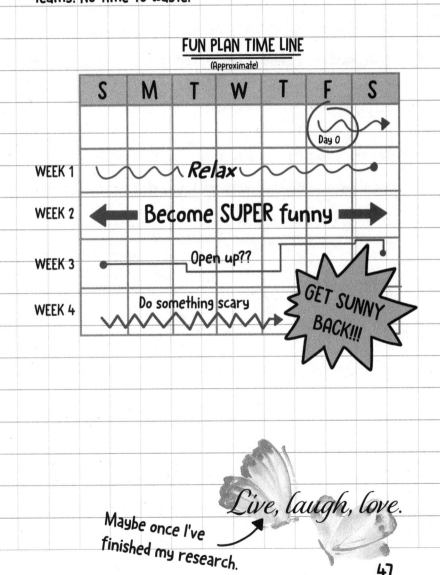

FUN PLAN TIME LINE
(Approximate)

S	M	T	W	T	F	S
					Day 0	

WEEK 1 — Relax

WEEK 2 — Become SUPER funny

WEEK 3 — Open up??

WEEK 4 — Do something scary

GET SUNNY BACK!!!

Live, laugh, love.

Maybe once I've finished my research.

47

My experiment is OFFICIALLY in action! Today I'm going to master the first element of my theory, a.k.a. the art of relaxation. According to the dictionary, "relaxation" is defined as "a state of being free from tension or anxiety." Easy. Maybe.

I'm going to sit really still, clear my mind, relax all my muscles, and BECOME relaxed. I read that drawing spirals helps too, so I'll throw in a few of those. Starting now.

9:14 a.m.

Obstacle detected: Juniper just came downstairs, and I can smell her toxic fumes from across the room. For

48

the past two years, she's been trying to get an audition for this TV show called <u>Teen Survival Challenge</u>. In order to "practice the art of wilderness survival," she only showers once a month.

I'm going to try breathing through my mouth only.

9:18 a.m.

Juniper sat next to me and started sharpening her spear.

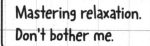 Mastering relaxation.
Don't bother me.

 It looks like you're holding in a fart.

YOU'RE a fart.

I would have had a better comeback if I'd had a little more time.

Juniper just went outside, thankfully. Back to relaxation. I feel like it's going to work now.

9:29 a.m.

I got a glimpse of my reflection in the window, and FYI, I don't think I look like I'm holding in a fart.

9:34 a.m.

Okay, I'm starting to get the hang of relaxation

The house has been breached! Juniper tried to throw her spear at a squirrel and hit the kitchen window, which would've shattered if she were better at throwing things. My mom went outside, and the yelling has probably reached 150 decibels.

HOW AM I SUPPOSED TO RELAX IN THIS ENVIRONMENT?

10:45 a.m.

My mom came back in a huff and said that since I was "just sitting around" on my phone, I should go with her to NASA to help with some kind of make-your-own-astronaut-ice-cream workshop. Then she started doing that annoying thing where she elbows me and says, "Let's get you out of the house!" I explained that I was in the middle of important research and that going to the workshop would be 0% valuable and also 0% fun.

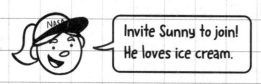

Invite Sunny to join! He loves ice cream.

Astronaut ice cream isn't even real ice cream. He wouldn't want to come.

I didn't want my mom to ask any more questions, so I said I would go. I don't need her or really anyone to know what happened with Sunny. I just need to finish my research, and then everything will go back to normal. Probably.

11:03 a.m.

Observation: Lifting boxes is incompatible with relaxation.

11:24 a.m.

Being around screaming children who want (fake) ice cream is also incompatible with relaxation.

52

NASA Cafeteria Kitchen

Gross

Tantrum zone

Fake ice cream
demonstration area

11:40 a.m.

Guess who just showed up to the workshop? That girl Lada
with the long ponytail.

She sat down next to me and asked where the ice
cream was. I promised my mom I wouldn't "be critical,"
but it just sort of slipped out that there is no ice
cream here, only astronaut ice cream, a.k.a. lies,
a.k.a. a freeze-dried pile of chemicals that no actual
astronaut has ever taken to space. Lada didn't seem
to care, because she immediately started mixing

53

ingredients without even washing her hands. Or
clearing her station!

I'm trying to focus on relaxing, but I'm very distracted
by the fact that Lada isn't listening to any of my
mom's instructions. Or measuring anything. And there
are bits of dried egg white all over her ponytail. I
mentioned that there's a measuring cup if she wanted
to be more precise about her cream of tartar, but she
said she would rather "let the winds of life" lead her.

She should probably
wear a hairnet

Way too much
cream of tartar

Health code
violation

Lada pulled out a half-eaten bag of cheese bunnies from her sweater pocket and started crumbling them into her ice cream too. And then she ATE some!

It tastes like filth.

I thought my mom would be mad that Lada didn't follow the recipe, but instead she said that she admired Lada's creativity. Lada had a LOT of follow-up questions.

Do you think a cough drop would numb the flavor of the cheese bunnies?

What happens if I mix it for a very long time, such as a whole week?

My mom didn't really know the answer to any of her questions, but she suggested that Lada add a bunch of blue food coloring and freeze-dry it to see what happens. So now Lada is just waiting while my mom gives a presentation on the history of astronaut ice cream.

I should go back to relaxing.

Lada

What are you writing?

Me

I'm developing a super practical Theory of Fun.

I can't share the details because I haven't done enough supporting research yet. So it might be wrong.

Oh, okay.

Lada pulled out a book from her pocket called <u>The Apothecary's Daughter: Night of the Pox.</u> I guess that's all she wanted to know.

Lada

Theories are wrong all the time. People used to think they could cure all your diseases by putting bloodsucking leeches all over your body. But they were wrong! :)

Maple

Well, okay, this is what I have so far. I think there are 4 elements of fun: relaxation, humor, opening up, and doing something scary. If you master those 4 elements, you become fun.

I see.

Could the Theory of Fun be applied at school, like specifically in the lunchroom or at an extracurricular activity where you don't know anybody because you just moved here from a different country?

Good question. Theoretically, yes, it should work everywhere, including with a person's family, or with an old friend who isn't hanging out with you as much because they don't think you're very fun, for example.

I'm going to test all four elements on myself as the first human subject.

Fascinating.

12:08 p.m.

My mom told everyone it was time to check on their ice

creams in the freeze dryer, but Lada stayed back with me. She said that a good experiment should probably have at least two data points, and she volunteered HERSELF as the second subject.

I needed a minute alone to think about it, so that's what I'm doing right now.

Thoughts: I don't really know if I have the time to train a research assistant, especially when I only have 3.9 weeks to get Sunny back before Invention Convention team sign-ups. Then again, maybe having an assistant would speed things up a little? I think I'll ask Lada some questions about the scientific method to see if she's up to snuff.

12:36 p.m.

Well, it turns out Lada knows A LOT about the scientific method because her mom is an astrophysicist at NASA. So,

after a lot of careful consideration, I have decided that
Lada can join as my research assistant.

Theory of Fun Human Testing Consent Form

I, ___Lada___, agree to be a human subject in this
groundbreaking research experiment. If anything
horrible happens, I understand that it was completely
outside of Maple's control and she will not be
punished for it in any way. I also understand that I will
not be paid anything.

Signature: _____ ← Lada's signature?

12:48 p.m.

I've decided that since this is purely a professional and
probably temporary arrangement, there is no need to

61

mention my actual research objective, or anything related to Sunny.

I have to say, doing a research project with a research assistant is way less stressful than doing it alone. I told Lada that my previous attempts at mastering the art of relaxation had been unsuccessful, so now we're going to brainstorm new methods.

RELAXATION IDEAS

- Room full of puppies (100+)

Woof!   Woof!

- Massages every day (Lada demonstrated on my back, but it was very painful.)
- Make a lot of plans and cancel them (my idea)
- Take milk baths like they do in The Apothecary's Daughter Book 5: <u>The Sleeping Sickness</u>

full of milk

I'm not sure these ideas are very practical, except maybe the canceling-plans one. I bet Sunny would have some good ideas. I'd text him to ask, but I guess that kind of defeats the point. Also, I'd have to say, "This is Maple," since I'm not even sure his new phone has my number.

Lada is looking around at the materials we have on hand, including all the contents of her pockets. There are a LOT more cheese bunnies in there.

1:32 p.m.

Interruption: My mom took the fake astronaut ice creams out of the freeze dryer.

Lada's ice cream. Looks like something a blueberry might throw up.

Lada hasn't said anything in a while. She keeps staring at the ice cream and rubbing her chin. I'm really glad she's not going to eat it. I think she would at a minimum get horrible diarrhea.

Oh, Lada just ate it. Maybe I agreed too soon about having her as my research assistant?

Never mind, I'm now CERTAIN that taking on Lada as my research assistant was a brilliant move because she just had a genius idea. She said the chalky texture of the ice cream reminded her of a bath bomb she once got for Hanukkah, and we could probably make our own with the ingredients we already have here! Brilliant!

Lada's bath bomb. Shaped like a dreidel.

I looked it up, and here's what you need to make a bath bomb:

64

CHECKLIST	
1. 4 tablespoons cream of tartar	☑
2. 1/2 cup Epsom salts (Lada thinks table salt is fine.)	☑
3. Food coloring (specifically the blue and green ones)	☑
4. A mold for the bath bomb (I took a couple of my mom's plastic rockets from the car. I'm sure she won't notice.)	☑
5. 1 cup baking soda (Lada just grabbed some from the custodian's closet.)	☑
6. Rubbing alcohol (I have a whole bottle in my first aid kit. And another in my backup first aid kit!)	☑

This is where we poured the mixture into the molds! Observations: It was really easy to squish the mixture into the molds because once we combined all the ingredients, they kind of solidified into a squishy putty. Like play dough but for scientists.

This is where Lada accidentally squirted the food coloring all over her sweater. I hope it comes out.

The bath bombs turned out extremely well in my opinion.

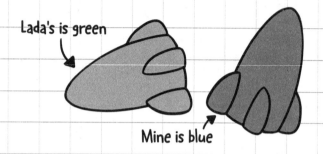

Lada's is green

Mine is blue

My bath bomb was a little fragile, so I triple-wrapped it in my sweater and buckled it into the middle seat (the safest seat in the car) before we drove home. When my mom asked about my "new friend," I said, "That's my sweater wrapped around a bath bomb." My mom clarified that she was talking about Lada. Oh, of course.

I explained that Lada and I have a PURELY professional relationship, and she's just my research assistant for an ongoing experiment and in NO way a replacement for Sunny. My mom said that new friends don't have to replace old friends, and that it looked like Lada and I were having "lots of fun over there." That's highly unlikely, seeing as we haven't actually mastered any of the elements of fun yet.

Lada and I made a detailed outline for how we'll test the bath bombs at our own homes:

BATH INSTRUCTIONS

1. Draw a bath to exactly 99° Fahrenheit.
2. Place the bath bomb exactly <u>three inches</u> from faucet.
3. Play the exact same song called "Ocean Sounds Premium (calming)."
4. Get into the bath.
5. Set timer for exactly fifteen minutes.
6. Exit bath.
7. Record findings <u>IMMEDIATELY</u>.

It's time.

I'm about to get into the bath. Just FYI, there were three versions of "Ocean Sounds Premium (calming)" available, so let's just hope the 2009 remaster is the correct one.

Oops, the bath just went to 99.3°. I need to run a little bit of cold water to get it back to 99°, which several bathtub-manufacturing websites have claimed is the perfect bath temperature.

Update: I've just completed step 2 and placed the bath bomb three inches from the faucet. It's fizzing as expected.

Update: I'm pressing play now. I will report back in exactly 15 minutes, maybe 16 depending on dry time.

ALERT:
THE EXPERIMENT HAS BEEN COMPROMISED!

About four minutes in, I noticed that my hand looked blue, which probably meant that it was low on blood circulation. I naturally responded by doing a few arm circles to get the blood flowing again. But THEN I noticed that my arm was blue too. THEN I noticed that my entire body was blue, all the way up to my nose!

Why did I think it was a good idea to put my chin into the water and blow bubbles? I can't go to school like this. I'll definitely turn 100% red from embarrassment . . . and I'm already 100% blue . . . which means I'll be 100% purple!

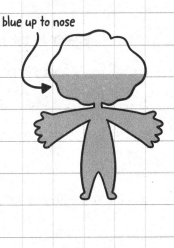

blue up to nose

69

And people like Jared will call me Murple! Sunny will be too embarrassed to even be seen with me.

I'm trying to scrub the blue off, but nothing is working. I need to get to my first aid kit STAT, because there are several ointments in there that might fix this.

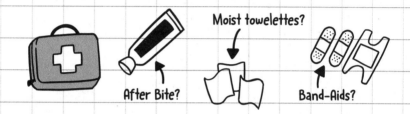

After Bite?

Moist towelettes?

Band-Aids?

8:38 p.m.

I passed Juniper in the hallway, and she told me I look like one of those blue people from Appalachia. I told her it was obviously just a side effect of my bath bomb, but Juniper said to look it up. I'm not looking that up.

Okay, I'm looking it up.

what is Appalachia

Blue People

who are the blue people of Appalachia

Yes, the Blue People Are Real!

how do blue people become blue

is caused by a rare blood condition, ofte married his aunt, which resulted in

I don't have any aunts. Maybe there's another way??

what are other causes for blue skin

how do you live with this condition

can you infect other people with blue

is my family safe

will my snot be blue

will my poop be blue **???**

Oh no, THREE YEARS AGO I ate a slice of blue ice cream cake, and I think my poop came out kind of blue. AND my lips turned blue. Is that where I first caught the blue disease?

~~Dear world,~~

~~If you are reading this, it's because I have not made it. I~~
~~would like the world to take up my important research,~~
~~since I know it's much greater than me. I would like to~~
~~give all of my possessions to my family except Juniper. I~~
~~don't want her to get anything. And my geode should go~~
~~to Sunny because it's actually his and I forgot to tell him~~
~~I had it. Please also tell him that I'm sorry I died still~~
~~unfun. . . . I was working on it.~~

~~Goodbye.~~

~~P.S. Please scatter my ashes in space as I have requested~~
~~multiple times.~~

9:30 a.m.

Please disregard my goodbye letter. It looks like it was a food-dye issue after all, because I sweated most of the blue off onto my sheets. I'm still alive.

9:36 a.m.

Someone just rang the doorbell. I didn't even know we had a doorbell.

11:20 a.m.

Update: It was Lada!

And she was COMPLETELY GREEN except for one skin-colored splotch on her face. Apparently, Lada's mom found my mom's address in the NASA directory. Since they only live 1.2 miles away, Lada just walked here!

She showed me all her findings from last night. It seemed like it went similarly to mine except that as far as I know, Lada didn't write a goodbye letter. I guess she used that time to figure out the recipe for a bath-bomb antidote, which she brought with her. It smelled like vinegar, but she demonstrated on her face, and it did, in fact, work. Now she has TWO skin-colored splotches on her face. I don't think she was bothered by being green.

= green

non-green splotch

We decided to have an official debriefing (like they do in the CIA after a big mission) to figure out where exactly we went wrong.

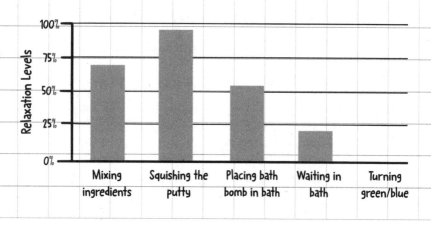

This is why human testing is so important, because you never really know how theories will work in the real world. It wasn't the bath bomb itself that helped us relax—it was the squishy putty!

We should make lots and lots of putty!

We went to the kitchen, and Lada immediately started opening up cabinets and throwing ingredients into a bowl like she'd been in our kitchen before. My mom poked her head in and said, "You go, girls!" but I told Lada to ignore her. Pretty soon we had a HUGE batch.

We did all kinds of testing with it, including:

Throwing it onto the window

SPLAT!

Spinning it like pizza dough

Sitting on it to make tooting noises (I know that's immature, but we only did it twice. Each.)

TOOT!

Squishing it onto Lada's face (This turned out to be hazardous when a little bit went up her nose.)

Lada thought we should name our invention Relaxigoo, but we ultimately decided to go for something more scientific: Relaxium.

Now we're in business. The business of fun!

1:32 p.m.

I have to say that every time I squish the Relaxium in my hand, I feel at least 3% more relaxed. I'm going to 3D-print a couple of containers tonight so that we can bring Relaxium with us EVERYWHERE, like more specifically to school. And even more specifically to the classes I have with Sunny.

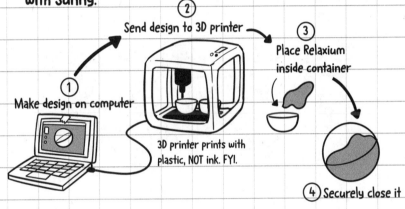

① Make design on computer

② Send design to 3D printer

3D printer prints with plastic, NOT ink. FYI.

③ Place Relaxium inside container

④ Securely close it

8:04 p.m.

My mom asked me why the bathtub was blue, but I said I had no idea.

How am I just "possible" if I'm definitely already here?

Don't say "impossible." Say "I'm possible."

77

I'm pretty sure Sunny's not even going to recognize me at school because I'll be SO relaxed. I thought about it all last night while the containers were printing: I'm going to squish the Relaxium, casually walk by his locker, and say, "Sup." I'm not even going to text him first.

8:22 a.m.

SUNNY ISN'T AT SCHOOL TODAY!

I mean, Sunny isn't at school today. Using a period instead of an exclamation point because I'm so relaxed. No big deal. I'll just say "sup" tomorrow. Totally chill.

Oh no, it's Discussion Day in social studies. If we want full participation points, we have to say at least one thing. I know talking in class shouldn't be as scary as objectively worse threats like the sun exploding, but it's still one of my top ten Earth fears.

Ms. Mupps asked us to answer this question: What is Leonardo da Vinci's most significant invention and why?

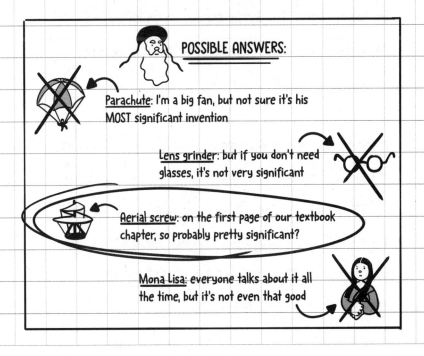

POSSIBLE ANSWERS:

<u>Parachute</u>: I'm a big fan, but not sure it's his MOST significant invention

<u>Lens grinder</u>: but if you don't need glasses, it's not very significant

<u>Aerial screw</u>: on the first page of our textbook chapter, so probably pretty significant?

<u>Mona Lisa</u>: everyone talks about it all the time, but it's not even that good

I think I should play it safe and say the aerial screw, since it probably influenced the modern helicopter, which is really important for people in remote locations getting to the hospital in an emergency. It probably also influenced the modern screw, right?

1:40 p.m.

Oh no, Ovi Nagar just said that HIS favorite invention is the "twirly machine." Ms. Mupps clarified that he must be talking about the aerial screw, which influenced the modern helicopter. That's what I was going to say!

1:46 p.m.

Maybe I should go back to the parachute. I could say it's really important because it lets astronauts land safely back on Earth. Or, wait, I'm not sure we would even HAVE astronauts if we didn't have telescopes, which use lenses, which probably require the lens grinder. Should I say that?

1:51 p.m.

SAY SOMETHING

There's only ten minutes left in class. I'm just going to say that the lens grinder was "very significant."

1:59 p.m.

I was going to raise my hand, but Mahogany Perez kept on talking for five minutes about how helicopters are vastly superior to the Mona Lisa. I'm not sure how to link THAT back to the lens grinder.

2:05 p.m.

I almost forgot about the Relaxium! Getting it now!

sweat droplets

81

I DID IT. I squished the Relaxium, raised my hand, and said I agreed with Mahogany's comment. And then the bell rang.

Wow, thank goodness for this Relaxium.

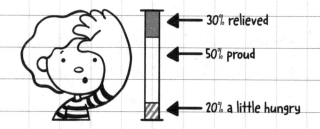

30% relieved

50% proud

20% a little hungry

I bet this is how Jackie Grand felt when the International Space Station module depressurized and she had to use floating potato chips to locate the source of the air leak, and SHE SAVED EVERYONE ON BOARD.

I told Lada about my recent relaxation breakthrough as soon as I saw her in computer science.

We had to do a discussion in social studies, and it was a real asteroid field out there. No one raising their hands, no time limits—real chaos. I was almost ready to give up my participation points and call it a day, but I squished my trusty Relaxium and pulled through with a pretty good comment.

Lada agreed that it was definitive proof that Relaxium REALLY works. She asked if that meant it was time to cross relaxation off the list, since she had participated in class a lot today too. Maybe too much. And then we could move on to mastering humor?

Well, maybe we should try testing the Relaxium in multiple different scenarios, just to make sure it REALLY works.

I just want to make sure that Sunny sees me at peak relaxation, although I didn't really want to get into the details with Lada. Luckily, she agreed to continue our testing phase without asking any questions. She's really shaping up to be a great assistant.

3:43 p.m.

Do I look relaxed?

Yes. Do I look relaxed?

Not really

Do I look like I'm holding in a fart?

No

Okay, phew.

Tuesday, 8:01 a.m.

Sunny isn't here again today, so I guess we'll have to wait a little longer to cross off relaxation. I wonder if I should text him to see if he's okay?

8:14 a.m.

He probably just has a cold.

8:20 a.m.

But what if it's something more serious, like a brain-eating amoeba?

11:42 a.m.

Sunny probably doesn't have a brain-eating amoeba.

⚠ WARNING

Brain-eating amoeba will eat your brain, causing DEATH!!

2:33 p.m.

Although, what if he does? What if the lake near his

house is actually contaminated and an amoeba crawled up his nose?

He probably doesn't have a brain-eating amoeba.

BUT WHAT IF HE DOES?

Phew, Sunny's back in school today. He told Mr. Wormley he had bronchitis so he couldn't do even one page of his homework.

Lada and I should figure out a super-relaxed way to walk so that we can casually walk through the halls between classes. And maybe we'll pass by Sunny's locker too.

Lada came up with a walk based heavily on a rhythmic gymnastics routine she did in fourth grade. I thought it was a little much, so I suggested a couple of tweaks. Now it looks like this:

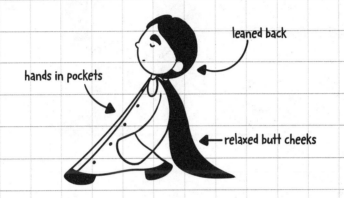

9:56 a.m.

UPDATE: I just walked by Sunny's locker using my new walk:

That couldn't have BEEN more relaxed.

Building off our walking success, Lada showed me an extremely chill (although potentially risky) way to sit in your chair.

45°

I'm going to wait until Sunny looks over here and give it a shot

I almost fell out of my chair! But then Sunny said, "Nice save." I think he's noticing.

My bus got in at the same time as Sunny's, so we ended up walking into school together. I didn't want to waste this chance to talk to him since we haven't really spoken in almost two weeks, but I also didn't want to say the wrong thing. I squished the Relaxium, and the most **PERFECT** conversation starter just rolled out.

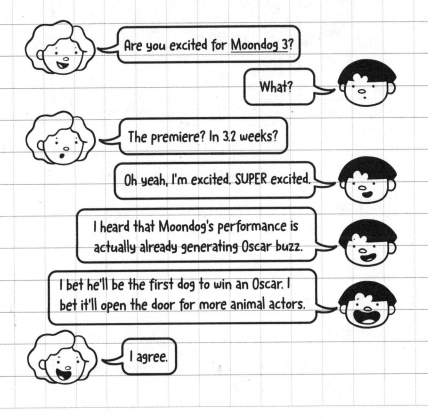

Are you excited for <u>Moondog 3</u>?

What?

The premiere? In 3.2 weeks?

Oh yeah, I'm excited. SUPER excited.

I heard that Moondog's performance is actually already generating Oscar buzz.

I bet he'll be the first dog to win an Oscar. I bet it'll open the door for more animal actors.

I agree.

Then the bell rang. I would say that was HIGHLY successful. I know it wasn't the longest conversation in the history of conversations, but I feel like it was a really good start. As Jackie Grand always says:

"The first step to getting to the moon is getting out of bed."
— Jackie Grand

poster in my room

I've just got to trust the process—the experiment is working!

10:48 a.m.

I'm at the Maker Lab to work on my computer science project, which is a weather website that tells you if it's raining outside. And guess what? Someone fixed the E key on my computer! Today is looking like a pretty good day, maybe even 4 out of 5 stars.

I don't even mind that Ovi keeps on asking me how to take a screenshot on the computer (he really needs to learn how to google stuff), or that Mahogany has completely copied me by getting a journal. (Hers is VERY fuzzy and probably 100% full of love letters to Lars Ip.) I'm so relaxed, I'm even going to design some extreme-weather icons for my website.

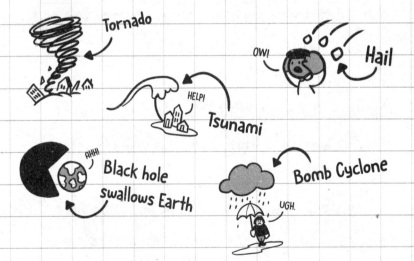

(Not even worried about any of these. Suuuuper unlikely. Probably.)

10:50 a.m.

Sunny, Jared, and the karate crew just came into
the Maker Lab. Maybe Sunny wants to continue our
conversation from earlier?

10:51 a.m.

Oh, they're just here to play Dinotown on the computer.
It's fine, I'm SUPER busy with my weather website anyway.

10:53 a.m.

Sunny just shouted my name. I'm going over there.

11:12 a.m.

Update: That was a **HORRIBLE** mistake. What was I
thinking, going over there when I'm only 25% fun???!!

Sunny wanted my input because he and Jared were
arguing about who would win in a fight, a velociraptor
or a Roomba. Sunny thought I would be a good

tiebreaker because I know "ALL the facts." It sort of seemed like he was giving me a chance to redeem myself in front of Jared. I'm not going to lie: I felt a LOT of pressure.

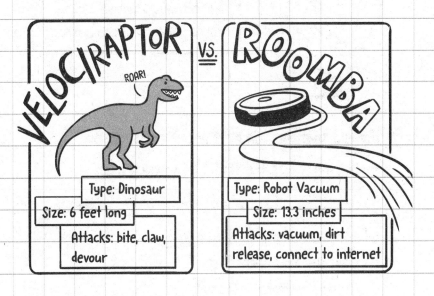

Jared thought Roombas would win because "they're sick," which wasn't a real reason. Sunny thought velociraptors because they could flip the Roomba upside down with their one long claw. I wished I didn't have to answer in front of Jared and everyone from the karate squad. Then again, I'd had pretty good luck with the Relaxium this week, so I just squeezed it and said my answer:

I don't have enough data so my answer is: inconclusive.

I thought that was the best possible response, considering it was the truth. Sunny disagreed.

Come onnnnnn, Maple! Break the tieeeeeeee!!!!!

I decided to say Roomba because it has access to the internet, which is the greatest weapon ever. But then I changed my mind, because the internet didn't exist in the time of dinosaurs. But then again, if it was multiple Roombas, maybe they could electrocute the velociraptor together. But then again . . .

Jared interrupted me.

Obviously the Roomba, because it took Maple so long to decide and now the dinosaurs are extinct!

EVERYONE laughed, including Sunny. Even Mahogany Perez laughed, and I'm pretty sure she was too far away to even hear what we were talking about.

I could feel my face turning at least 66% red. I didn't realize I was supposed to be FUNNY

Roombas win!

in my answer; otherwise I would've approached the question very differently! I would have said something REALLY funny like . . . well . . . I can't think of anything RIGHT NOW, but that's because we haven't moved on to humor yet! I need to find Lada ASAP.

11:47 a.m.

I didn't have Lada's phone number, so I had to look all over the school for her. I found her in the last place I would ever go, which is the school track. I didn't even know we had a track. She was power walking in circles WHILE reading her book, The Apothecary's Daughter: Death by Daybreak.

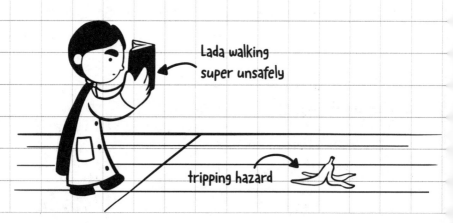

Lada walking
super unsafely

tripping hazard

I told Lada that she should pat herself on the back because we'd finished relaxation. Yay! Time to move on to humor **RIGHT NOW**.

Lada started nodding a bunch, which I think meant she was ready and excited. She thought we should have a special ceremony where we wrote "relaxation" on a piece of paper and then burned it.

I think this is what Lada was thinking?

We didn't have matches, though, so Lada just did a quick interpretive dance and crossed relaxation off our list.

1. ~~Relax~~

2. Have a sense of humor

3. Open up

4. Do something scary

No more celebrating. I told Lada we had to get serious about humor STAT so we could come up with a strategy to make EVERYONE laugh.

Lada had a lot of follow-up questions.

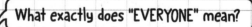

What exactly does "EVERYONE" mean?

Everyone in the whole state? Room?

What if there are 50 people in the room and only 49 laugh?

What if one person has laryngitis so they can't laugh but they wanted to?

I told Lada that 49 out of 50, a.k.a. 98% of a room, seemed good enough, although maybe some people count more than others, like for example if we've known them for 7.2 years.

That seemed to satisfy her, because she put away her book and said, "Let the HAHAs begin!" Then I got her phone number so I wouldn't have to come ALL the way out to the track again.

2:38 p.m.

Okay, I've got it. Who would win between a Roomba and a velociraptor? Oh, I'm sorry, did I say "Room-ba"? I meant "Room-BYE"!

VELOCIRAPTORS WIN! Take that, Jared.

RIP
Died from
Maple's
hilarious joke

same cause of death

Lada and I spent the first half of computer science messaging ideas back and forth for our humor research. Here's the plan: We're going to record the funniest things we see and organize them in a scientific chart. Then we can figure out EXACTLY what makes the funniest things funny.

EVENT	HA LEVEL	HUMOR TYPE
Internet image of a potato pooping out fries	HAHAHA	Silly, potty humor, surprise, clever
Juniper sprayed me unexpectedly with water and started laughing	HAHA (for her)	Surprise, enjoying the suffering of others
Dog crowd-surfing video	HAHAHA	Surprise, animals
Ovi called Mr. Wormley "Daddy" by accident	**HAHAHA**	Someone messing up, silly
Poster in science I can't help that I'm a FUN GUY!	HAHAHA	Pretty clever
Mahogany showed us a video of a man shouting "PANCAKES" to strangers on the street. We didn't laugh, but Mahogany laughed really hard AND it has 38 million views.	HAHAHA?	Surprise, silly, everybody else laughed

100

There are obviously many paths to achieving a HAHAHA ranking, although it's tough to say which type of humor is the most effective. Lada thinks it's probably silliness, but I'm not sure. When Jared said that thing about the dinosaurs going extinct, it wasn't really silly. Or thaaat clever. Or related to potty humor. I don't know which is the best approach.

While I was waiting on the front lawn for the bus, Lada showed me how to do a headstand. She said it would help get more blood flowing to our brains so we could think a little harder. I can't say it really helped me come up with any ideas, although it did make me pretty dizzy.

I take it back—maybe there IS something to it! Lada and I tried the headstands again, and right when we were upside down, Sunny and his friends walked by on their way to karate practice laughing REALLY hard about something. I suggested to Lada that we spy on them, since clearly there was some HAHAHA material going on that we should probably observe. Lada got excited about that and put on her "spy" sunglasses.

4:06 p.m.

We're in position.

Jared Grody called someone on his cell phone, and I guess it was his dad because he said, "Hello, Mr. Grody," in a pretend deep voice.

We've kidnapped your son. You must send 30 pizzas to . . .

Sunny, what's your address?

whispers that I cannot hear

211 Timber Way! Oh and also we need two sides of mozzarella dippers! OKAY, BYE!

EVERYBODY laughed. Even Lada and I chuckled a little, although quietly so we wouldn't give our hiding spot away. Our next step seemed pretty clear to me: we should do a prank.

Surprisingly, Lada did NOT agree. She said she wished she could take her laughter back because it's "pure evil" to trick someone like that. I agreed that it's kind of evil to trick someone who doesn't deserve it . . . but what if we tricked someone who DOES deserve it? Like specifically my evil sister, Juniper? We could prank her, film it, show it in the Maker Lab, and then EVERYBODY would laugh (including Sunny).

Lada agreed that real, true evil should be punished. As long as Juniper REALLY deserved it, we should do it. I'm glad Lada's on board.

4:42 p.m.

I missed my bus so I had to call my mom to pick me up. She was not pleased.

4:59 p.m.

(Lada) < Great prank idea.

104

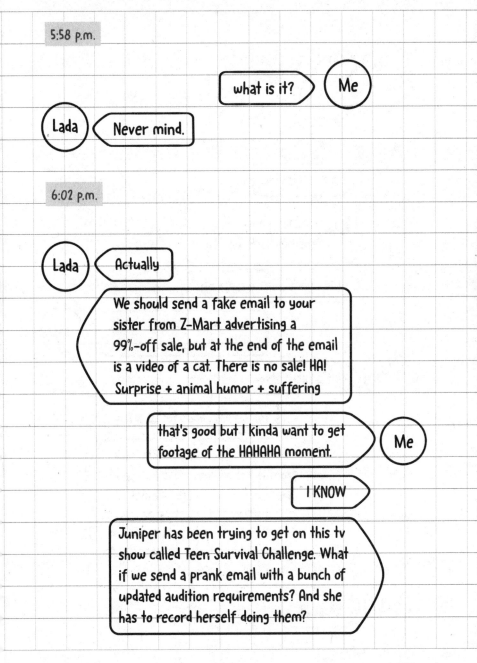

5:58 p.m.

Me: what is it?

Lada: Never mind.

6:02 p.m.

Lada: Actually

We should send a fake email to your sister from Z-Mart advertising a 99%-off sale, but at the end of the email is a video of a cat. There is no sale! HA! Surprise + animal humor + suffering

Me: that's good but I kinda want to get footage of the HAHAHA moment.

I KNOW

Juniper has been trying to get on this tv show called Teen Survival Challenge. What if we send a prank email with a bunch of updated audition requirements? And she has to record herself doing them?

105

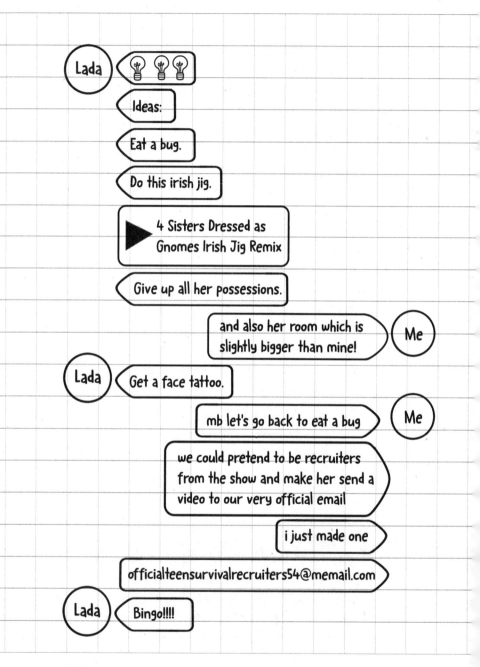

Friday, 11:30 a.m.

Lada came to the Maker Lab with me today at lunch.
We got the Teen Survival Challenge logo from the
internet, and I have to say, our email looks very
official. If the astronaut thing doesn't work out, maybe
I could be one of those people who send scam emails
to test people's cybersecurity skills? Hopefully not,
though—I'd rather be an astronaut.

To whom this may concern, which is Juniper:

The Teen Survival Challenge recruiting team
wishes to send you an updated requirement
should you audition for our show. All
candidates must prove that they can eat an
entire beetle, without the aid of water or soda.
We suggest that you practice a lot, should
you wish to be a part of our team. Video proof
is required by Saturday (tomorrow) at 3pm.

Sincerely,
The Recruiting Team

Sunny would think this is SO funny. Juniper once carved one of his best rocks into a sledgehammer, and he's never forgiven her.

(To be fair, Juniper didn't know that the pile of rocks was part of Sunny's collection, but she should've asked.)

Juniper was in a horrible mood when she got home, which I think means that she got the email. I invited Lada to come over tomorrow to observe the prank in real time, since I'm 99% sure Juniper will wait until the last possible second to do it.

I watched that pancake video a few more times, and it's starting to grow on me. I'm giving it an additional HA.

I'm kind of curious about what beetles taste like, so I'm looking it up.

Apparently, they are very nutritious. You also have to take off the arms and legs before you cook them. I wonder if I should send a follow-up email to Juniper just so she knows how to eat it safely?

Oh no.

AFRICAN LEAF BEETLE

Poison causes death by paralysis.

Well, those beetles live in the Kalahari Desert, so they're probably not in Texas. I'm not going to worry about it.

I've been thinking about this all night. African leaf beetles have wings, so they COULD fly here over the Atlantic Ocean. Or maybe they could board a ship. Or sneak into the mail! AND WE GET MAIL EVERY DAY! Except Sunday.

BUT STILL!

Maybe this prank is too risky.

When Lada got here, I showed her my recent findings about the African leaf beetle. I'm starting to get a little uneasy about the odds of this prank ending in a horrible disaster where we BOTH go to jail. Lada did some counter-research and concluded that we almost definitely don't have ANY African leaf beetles here, not even one. Still, she gave me her Relaxium and recommended I try the double squish.

It's not really helping. . . .

10:28 a.m.

Live updates: Juniper just went outside, and she brought two slices of bread. I think she's going to put the beetle into a sandwich. Lada brought binoculars, so we're trading off watching through the kitchen window.

10:32 a.m.

Juniper is digging around in the grass. Maybe she won't find a beetle?

10:34 a.m.

Oh, she just found one.

She put it into the sandwich. I can't tell what type it is! WHAT IF IT'S THE AFRICAN LEAF BEETLE?

10:35 a.m.

Now she's pacing back and forth! I'm starting to feel REALLY guilty. Should I maybe pull the plug?

10:40 a.m.

I whispered to Lada that Juniper isn't really that evil. She just doesn't shower that often. And that emergency flashlight she keeps stealing from me isn't even my favorite! Also, once, she cooked me toast when my parents weren't home, and it was pretty good! SHE DOESN'T DESERVE THIS!

Lada just opened the window and jumped out.

She's running to Juniper!

SHE KNOCKED THE SANDWICH OUT OF HER HAND!!!!!

Juniper was prettyyyy mad. We're fleeing to Lada's house!! Safety is in sight!

1:31 p.m.

Wow, Lada's house is AMAZING.

Dr. Katarina, Lada's mom, basically the coolest person EVER (after Jackie Grand). She's an astrophysicist at NASA!!!

Uncle Danish, Lada's uncle, a doctor, useful for questions about ankylosing spondylitis?

Uncle Belly, Lada's other uncle, doesn't have a job but has a podcast? Possibly the Juniper of the family?

When we came in, Dr. Katarina said that she'd heard ALL about me. Lada whispered something in Hungarian, but Dr. Katarina responded (in English):

I'm not embarrassing, right, Maple?

Absolutely not!

In addition to knowing a lot about dark matter, Dr. Katarina also knows a LOT about cheese. She has a whole drawer in the fridge completely stuffed with it. She made us a cheese board, which I learned is just a plate that you put cheese on.

Dr. Katarina told Uncle Belly to turn off his sitcoms because she wanted to hear all about our fun research. I should've told Lada that "top secret" generally means you can't tell ANYONE, including family. But I guess if your mom is a NASA astrophysicist, it's okay to bend the rules.

We told Dr. Katarina all about what happened with Juniper. I confessed that even though I was the one who wanted to do that prank in the first place, I was having serious doubts that anyone ever actually deserved prank punishment, including Juniper. But it was a huge bummer, because the prank clearly had a 100% laughter rate. I wasn't sure we were going to come up with anything as 100% successful as Jared's prank phone call.

 Well, why do you think you laughed when those other kids did their prank?

I started thinking about Jared's prank call. Why DID I laugh when he did that? I didn't really think the pizza trick was THAT funny. I guess I laughed because Lada laughed? But then Lada said that she didn't actually think it was funny either. She just laughed because I laughed!

Dr. Katarina started snapping her fingers and said, "Make the connection!" Clearly we were onto something BIG.

Maybe we were laughing because everyone else was laughing. . . .

Maybe laughter is funny?

Yeah, maybe it's contagious. Like a yawn.

snapping

Yes! Yes!

Maybe if you hear people laughing, anything can be funny! Even if you don't get it.

Like the laugh track on Uncle Belly's sitcoms! He laughs even though he doesn't understand the jokes.

I get some of them!

Maybe all we need is our own laugh track!

clap

Bingo. And THAT'S science!

clap

This is a GREAT discovery, because it shows that you don't have to be mean to conquer humor. You don't even have to be FUNNY! You just need to have background laughter. Lada and I agreed that what we need is to build a portable laugh track. Then, instead of having to find the perfect joke, we'll just play the laugh track whenever we say something sort of funny, and it'll make EVERYONE laugh.

Uncle Belly let us borrow a couple of handheld recorders that he uses for his podcasts. We had to promise that we would give them back in "mint condition," a.k.a. not even a scratch.

Then we got Lada's whole family to laugh on cue so we could record it. We had to do a couple of takes, though, because I think people were laughing a little too hard on purpose.

Lada thought the laugh track would probably be more effective if nobody could see where it was coming from. I had a TON of ideas for ways to disguise the recorder, but I got interrupted with a text from my mom.

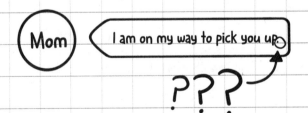

She ended her text with a period. That ALWAYS means that she's mad about something.

I found out in the car that Juniper told her all about the prank email, and my mom thought it was very "untasteful." When we got home, I had to go to my room to think about what I did. I thought this was an enormous waste of time, seeing as I'd already thought about it at Lada's house and vowed to abandon pranks, but my mom didn't agree.

5:10 p.m.

I watched the pancake video a few more times on my phone and played the laugh track right after the man said "PANCAKES." The laugh track definitely makes it funnier.

5:24 p.m.

My mom took away my phone so I could "reflect a little harder," but she didn't do anything about my computer.

Lada (I hid the recorder in my pocket and played the laugh track

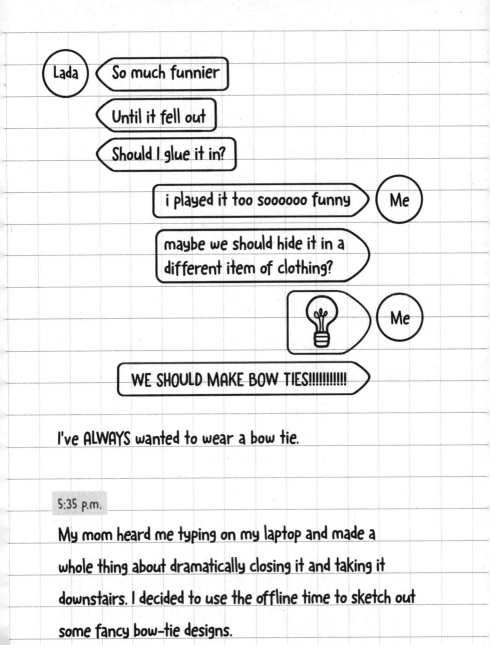

Lada — So much funnier

Until it fell out

Should I glue it in?

i played it too soooooo funny — **Me**

maybe we should hide it in a different item of clothing?

💡 — **Me**

WE SHOULD MAKE BOW TIES!!!!!!!!!!!

I've ALWAYS wanted to wear a bow tie.

5:35 p.m.

My mom heard me typing on my laptop and made a whole thing about dramatically closing it and taking it downstairs. I decided to use the offline time to sketch out some fancy bow-tie designs.

121

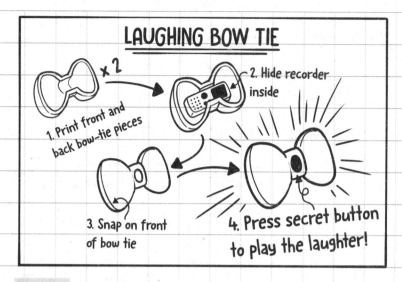

LAUGHING BOW TIE

x 2

1. Print front and back bow-tie pieces

2. Hide recorder inside

3. Snap on front of bow tie

4. Press secret button to play the laughter!

5:56 p.m.

I practiced saying random things and playing the laugh track. It's just SO FUNNY. Sunny's going to love this.

I'll take those eggs . . . scrambled!

HAHA HAHAHAHA HA HAHA HAHAHA HA

I realized I wouldn't get my computer back until I did something drastic, so I went downstairs and told Juniper I was EXTREMELY sorry. The events that occurred this morning will not be repeating themselves EVER, especially now that I've learned that pranks are stupid. I hoped she would consider forgiving me, especially since we did ultimately save her from getting poisoned by the African leaf beetle.

Juniper said she would forgive me if I helped her dehydrate some mango slices for her wilderness trail mix.

Not helping

I bet my mom will at least give me my computer back after I finish dehydrating these mangos.

7:15 p.m.

Knew it! Got my computer AND phone back. I'm designing the laughing bow ties, and I think I can print at least two of them tonight!

This is turning out to be really good practice for the Invention Convention. This bow tie is way more complicated than anything I've ever 3D-printed before, including that rock display case I made with Sunny.

Update: The bow ties look REALLY fancy. Possibly even MEGA-FANCY. Maybe one day I could make some of these for the astronauts at NASA? I'm sure they could use a laugh in space.

4:41 p.m.

I sent Lada pictures of the finished bow ties, and she says we HAVE to wear them to school tomorrow. Lada wanted to try them out in the Maker Lab at lunch, but I was a little concerned that the Maker Lab wouldn't have the optimal audience. Some people don't go there every day, like for example the karate team, and more specifically Sunny. I suggested we try it in science class.

Lada: Will we get in trouble?

Me: maybe . . .

but sometimes you have to break a few eggs if you want to make an omelet

Lada: ?

Me: you have to break some rules to get the reward

Lada: Ohhhhhhhhh

6:03 p.m.

I love wearing my bow tie. I think I'm going to wear one all the time, even when I don't have to be funny.

Lada and I texted all last night, and here's the plan: I'm going to ask Mr. Wormley to go over question two from last night's science worksheet. After he goes over 2a, he'll have to go over 2b. And then Lada is supposed to blurt out "or not 2b," which according to Lada is a really famous line from a play. And then we both press the laugh track. It's going to be SO funny.

8:06 a.m.

Lada met me at my locker to pick up her bow tie. I have to say, we look amazing.

paparazzi

127

I hope Sunny doesn't have bronchitis again.

8:11 a.m.

Sunny just walked into science. The plan is a go!

8:33 a.m.

I'm going to raise my hand as soon as Sunny and Titus

stop whispering. I don't want to start the plan until

they're paying attention.

8:40 a.m.

Do you still want to do it?

Yes, just waiting for the right moment.

We can do it later in the Maker Lab if you'd rather.

No, I can do it.

Can I just borrow your Relaxium?

Just executed the double squish, and I feel the power

of the Relaxium already. Mr. Wormley told Titus and

Sunny to stop whispering and pay attention. It's now or never. I'm raising my hand!

8:46 a.m.

The plan is in motion! I asked Mr. Wormley to go over question two, and he said, "Sure thing!"

8:48 a.m.

He's going over 2a. 2b is next!

8:50 a.m.

Oh no. He moved on to 2b, but he never SAID "2b," which is essential for our joke. I was worried that I messed it all up, so I raised my hand again and asked him:

When you get a chance, can you please say specifically whether you are working on part 2a or 2b?

The second part.

NOOOOO. WHAT DO I DO?

8:52 a.m.

I'm going to ask again, but maybe just word it like "Can you please say the words '2a' or '2b' with regards to what problem you are doing?"

8:53 a.m.

Okay, I'm raising my hand. But Lada is also raising HER hand?? The plan is falling apart!!!

9:04 a.m.

UPDATE: THE PLAN WAS A WILD SUCCESS!!

Mr. Wormley called on Lada, but instead of asking our question again, Lada just shouted:

PANCAKE!

Then she played her bow tie. There was a moment of silence. I didn't know what to do . . . so I played MY bow tie.

Then EVERYBODY LAUGHED, including Sunny.

Mr. Wormley couldn't tell where the laugh track was coming from. We just kept on playing our bow ties, and the class KEPT laughing. Eventually Mr. Wormley figured out it was us and made us hand in our bow ties. Usually I don't like getting in trouble, since I'm a little nervous that NASA will see it on my permanent record . . . but Lada promised me that her mom got in trouble ALL the time as a kid, and NASA still took her anyway. Plus, the look on Sunny's face made it totally worth it.

tear

Whew! Lada really saved me in there. She wasn't even SLIGHTLY mad that I messed up my part of the plan!

I think we did it!

1. ~~Relax~~

2. ~~Have a sense of humor~~

3. Open up

4. Do something scary

9:09 a.m.

Sunny came up to me after class and asked if we were making extra bow ties, because he realllyyyyyy wanted one. And would even pay! With a friends discount. Mahogany and Ovi wanted them too, but I said I might have to charge some people full price if I wanted to make

ANY profit. And the recorders would obviously not be
included.

I can't believe Sunny said "friends discount"! That means
he thinks we're friends again!!!!

Well, he didn't say "BEST friends discount." But I'm only
50% fun, so I just need to keep going. Still, I consider
this a HUGE breakthrough.

I let Lada know that people were interested in the
laughing bow ties, and we should probably go home
immediately and print 100 more. Lada thought this was

*Life isn't about the number
of breaths you take; it's
about the moments that
take your breath away.*

I'd rather take a lot of
breaths than have them
taken away. I looked it
up, and if you live to be
80, you'll take almost
700,000,000 breaths. I
plan to take at least
that many.

133

a great idea and came up with a whole global marketing strategy instead of paying attention in Spanish.

BUSINESS PLAN

CTO
Maple McNutt

CEO
Lada Quiche

PERKS PACKAGE

Private spaceship

Complimentary candy

Company-provided bow ties!

11:17 a.m.

We have AT LEAST thirty hours of printing to do, so Lada's going to need to come over for dinner. And maybe stay for breakfast. I called my mom to ask if I could have a friend over after school, and she said, "Sure! Do you and Sunny want mac and cheese?"

I informed her that it was actually Lada, not Sunny, but could we still have mac and cheese? She said, "Oh great! Awesome! Of course!" I'm glad there weren't too many follow-up questions.

I found a box of my dad's gold plastic rolls for the 3D
printer in the garage, so now we can make gold bow ties!
Lada thinks we could charge at least $50 per bow tie,
since we're not legally required to say that it's fake gold.
Although maybe I could knock $5 off for Sunny's friends
discount?

4:38 p.m.

Lada ALSO came up with a really clever name for our
company: Over the Rainbowtie™. I think there's a lot of
potential there.

OVER THE RAINBOWTIE™
HEADQUARTERS

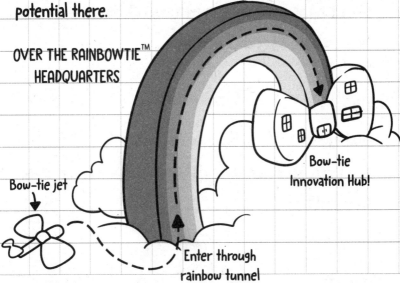

Bow-tie jet

Bow-tie
Innovation Hub!

Enter through
rainbow tunnel

Sunny would love this. Honestly, I think he would love hanging out with Lada. They both have TONS of ideas. They both LOVE making stuff. Maybe at some point we'll all hang out, just the three of us. Without Jared.

I should probably renegotiate the terms of our fun research to make Lada a 50-50 partner.

5:59 p.m.

My mom finished making the mac and cheese, and I have to say, today is shaping up to be at least a 4.7 out of 5 stars kind of day. Maybe even a 4.75? Putting my journal away so I don't get cheese on it!

6:01 p.m.

Just one more thing: the mac and cheese has BOW-TIE pasta in it. What are the odds? Definitely a 4.75 day. Okay, signing off now.

136

Bow-tie
pasta

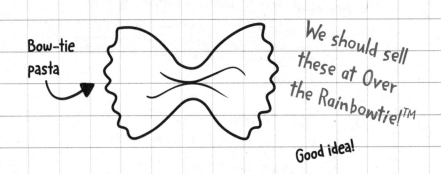

We should sell these at Over the Rainbowtie!™

Good idea!

7:02 p.m.

Update: Dinner did NOT go as planned.

We were about to sit down for dinner, and everything was basically perfect. Lada and I looked extra fancy in our bow ties. The mac and cheese was hot and gooey. We could only smell Juniper a little bit. Then my mom got a ding on her phone and checked her email.

That was the end of my 4.75-star day.

Apparently, Mr. Wormley emailed her ALL about the laughing bow ties, and it was not very positive.

This is a loose reconstruction of what the email PROBABLY said based on two witness accounts.

— ↗ X

Howdy, Daisy!

How ya doing? Do you like the weather? I'm just writing because Maple's laughing bow ties are a genius idea and they should probably win a Nobel Prize or at LEAST the Invention Convention. But alsoooo, I just wanted to add that she was super disruptive in class and I'm concerned, and I wanted to tell you so that the whole celebratory mac-and-cheese dinner would be ruined. Anyway, bye!

Sincerely,
Mr. Wormley

My mom got a stern look on her face and wanted to know what exactly he meant by these laughing bow ties. Lada and I agreed to do a brief demonstration, but I was pretty sure it wasn't going to go over like it did in class:

I was right. Zero HAs.

That's the least funny thing I've seen all year. And I saw that documentary about global warming.

I don't get it. You LOVE science. It's not like you to disrupt the class.

It's all part of our research experiment. We're learning how to scientifically become fun.

So that's what this bow-tie thing is? You're trying to be fun?

139

We're not just trying—we're succeeding. For your information, we're already 50% of the way there!

 LOL.

This doesn't concern you, Juniper.

 Maple, of course I want you to have fun, but there are so many other ways. You can go outside! Get off the computer! Or go see that Mooncat movie you and Sunny always talk about?

MoonDOG. And it's not even out yet.

 I'm organizing the Rocket Grrls lunar-eclipse dance party for next month at NASA. You both could help me make decorations! Or plan the playlist! There's plenty of ways to have fun without being disruptive.

Well, sorry, sometimes you have to disrupt the system if you want real change. I regret to inform you that our research is ONGOING.

141

And that was the end of dinner. I barely even got to eat any mac and cheese.

I don't know if I can fix it. And I promised Uncle Belly to give the recorder back in mint condition. And I hate breaking promises.

I can't believe they would yell at me like that IN FRONT OF LADA.

• 25% embarrassed

• 25% angry

• 25% disappointed

• 25% really worried about what Uncle Belly will say

Lada's family would never do that. Dr. Katarina would probably make us a cheese board to celebrate our

HUGE HUMOR BREAKTHROUGH.

It doesn't even matter, though, because my bow tie is destroyed. I don't know if I can ever be funny again without it. And if I can't be funny, then I don't know if I can ever really be 100% fun. And if I can't be 100% fun, then Sunny will never take me back. And also, it means Juniper was right, which is possibly the

WORST PART.

Lada just knocked on the door. I guess I should mention that I locked myself in the safe house, a.k.a. my closet, because I'm in no condition to speak to people right now, even my scientific partner. Or ex-scientific partner, I guess. She's probably knocking to tell me she doesn't want to do the research anymore after the horror show she witnessed at dinner.

SAFE HOUSE

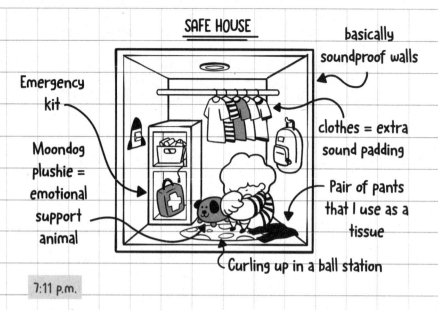

basically soundproof walls

Emergency kit

Moondog plushie = emotional support animal

clothes = extra sound padding

Pair of pants that I use as a tissue

Curling up in a ball station

7:11 p.m.

Lada slipped a piece of paper under the door.

1. % of the time that Juniper tells the truth = $(0/100 + 0/100 + 0/100 + 0/100)^{\text{infinity}}$ = 0%

2. If Juniper is correct 0% of the time and she says X, the inverse property tells us that X is NOT TRUE. Therefore, the opposite is always true. Which means that Maple's chances of being fun are 100%.

I told Lada through the door that I had some issues with her math. Given that we've only completed 2 out of 4

144

steps, a.k.a. 50% of the fun project, my chances of being fun are probably much closer to 50%.

Lada slipped another piece of paper under the door.

$$Lada = 50\%, Maple = 50\%$$
$$Lada + Maple = 100\%$$

I'm not sure if that math works out, but I opened the door a little so she could come in and show me her method.

7:18 p.m.

Lada asked if maybe this was a good time to move on to part 3 of our theory: "open up." I told Lada she should go first and then maybe I would go after. Lada agreed, but she made me promise to never ever spill her Super Secret. I assured her that nothing said in

145

the safe house leaves the safe house. The walls are basically soundproof. (But I would have to write her secret down for science.)

Lada's Super Secret:

When Lada was eight, she had a wart on her knee that wouldn't go away, even when she applied really powerful ointments to it. One day she went swimming in a lake.

—Wart

As she was climbing out of the water, her knee scraped the side of the dock, and the wildest thing happened. HER WART FELL OFF. And it just floated away in the lake.

When it was about five feet away, a herring, which is a species of fish, came out of nowhere and gulped it up. AND THEN, two days later, Uncle Danish caught a herring, and they grilled it and ate it for dinner.

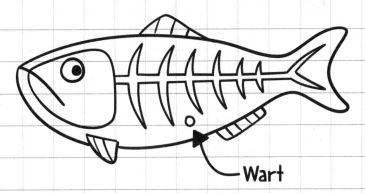

To this day, Lada wonders whether they all ate the fish that ate her wart. That's right. Lada's uncles possibly ate a little bit of their OWN NIECE.

I told Lada that this was a really big secret and I definitely wouldn't tell anyone. That's the kind of thing that social services could take her uncles away for.

It was my turn, but I couldn't think of any times that I had a wart. Lada said my secret didn't have to be gross like hers, but if it was, she was prepared. The only secret I could think of was:

Maple's Super Secret:

One time in class we were taking a spelling test, and I saw Mahogany Perez's answer for one of the questions. But I had already written my answer, so I didn't cheat or anything.

1. ~~Relax~~   3. ~~Open~~ up

2. ~~Have a sense of humor~~   4. Do something scary

I started to cross off "open up," but Lada said that maybe "opening up" meant talking about our deepest feelings, not just sharing Super Secrets. I disagreed.

Talking about secrets is pretty fun, but boring each other with our horrible, depressing feelings is basically the opposite of fun. Why would 83 out of 86 fun websites recommend opening up as fun if it was so obviously going to be unpleasant?

Because you have to break a few eggs to make an omelet.

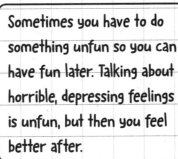

Sometimes you have to do something unfun so you can have fun later. Talking about horrible, depressing feelings is unfun, but then you feel better after.

I'm putting my pencil down to hear her out.

10:15 p.m.

So, according to Lada, there was this really old computer called the Enigma machine that was used to crack German code during World War II. It plays a large role in the Apothecary's Daughter, book 16: <u>A Nurse with No Name</u>. The reason the British needed the Enigma machine was because the German code changed every day, making it almost impossible to crack.

Enigma Machine

Lada thought we should invent something like the Enigma machine so only WE could decode each other's feelings. I liked the sound of that, especially the part where nobody else ever needed to know about our least-fun feelings. We decided to start brainstorming code ideas first thing tomorrow.

Uncle Belly came to pick Lada up, and she promised not to mention the broken recorder until I had more time to fix it.

10:17 p.m.

Now that I'm thinking more clearly, I can't believe Lada wants to keep doing the fun research with me, even though she saw me as Mople.

Mople

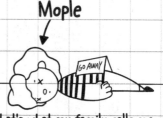

(That's what my family calls me when I'm feeling mopey.)

Nobody likes to hang out with Mople, not even me. Lada is probably the most patient person in the world.

10:31 p.m.

I'm really glad Lada moved here.

10:42 p.m.

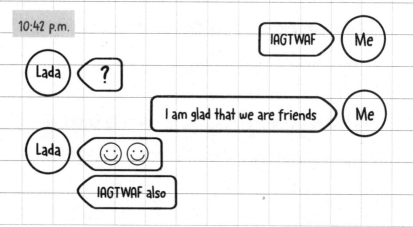

My mom seemed to think that the bow-tie breaking was punishment enough, because she was being really nice to me this morning and even asked if there was anything I wanted to talk to her about. I said no.

There's only 2.5 weeks left until it's time to sign up for Invention Convention teams, and Lada and I have a LOT of work to do if we want to get opening up finished in time. I'm thinking we spend a week on opening up and then we still have a whole week to do something scary. I think we can do it. Lada's really efficient, so I bet we can.

FUN PLAN TIME LINE

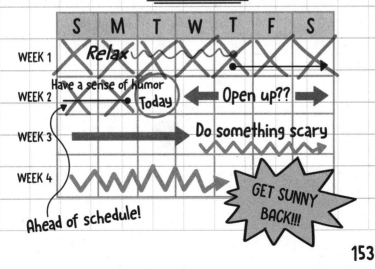

	S	M	T	W	T	F	S
WEEK 1		Relax					
WEEK 2	Have a sense of humor		Today	← Open up?? →			
WEEK 3	→				Do something scary		
WEEK 4							

Ahead of schedule!

GET SUNNY BACK!!!

Mr. Wormley handed out another worksheet today.

Inventions Unit: WS #2

Did you know that some of the greatest inventions were actually created by multiple people? List at least three. Please consider: How did these people work together? What skills did they each bring to the table?

1.) The International Space Station, which was built by many astronauts from multiple countries. Even though all the astronauts had different backgrounds, it actually made them a really good team because they all contributed different skills. Also, it didn't really matter that they all spoke different languages because space is a vacuum so sound doesn't carry at all.

2.) Google, which was created by Larry Page and Sergey Brin. They met in computer science class, which means they were both probably really good at computers. That is why they were a good team.

3.) The Jacuzzi, which was invented by the Jacuzzi brothers. Probably they weren't a good team because siblings fight all the time, but then maybe all the fighting made them need to relax, so they invented the Jacuzzi. Therefore, they were ultimately a good team.

154

I just had an idea.

I wonder if there's any way that me, Sunny, AND Lada could be a team of three for the Invention Convention. I know that's not EXACTLY what the pact says, but maybe we could add an extra part that includes Lada. I just think there's a really good chance, maybe even 99%, that Sunny and Lada would get along SUPER well, and I kind of think we'd maybe be the team to beat. Maybe I'm getting ahead of myself. I don't know if Lada would even want to do the Invention Convention with us. Going to think about it later.

11:12 a.m.

Lada and I are spending lunch in the Maker Lab researching different codes. Turns out there are a LOT of codes out there. Some of them are clever, but honestly most of them are really silly. Like this one called pig latin that has nothing to do with pigs or Latin. You just move the first sound to the end of the word and add an "ay" after every word.

FOOD = OODFAY MO...

DOG = OGDAY   SHIRT = ...

EGG = EGGWAY   CAT= ATCAY

Mahogany just overheard our discussion and said, "Is that pig latin? I mean, igpay atinlay?" We definitely need to come up with something more sophisticated.

11:28 a.m.

Lada found another code called Openglopish, where you add an "op" before every vowel sound. So, for example,

Jackie Grand would be Jopackopie Gropand. This is very silly.

Juniper just texted me.

Juniper

hey hey, sorry bout the bow tie, dweeb.

Juniper

Dear Maple, I am extremely sorry about breaking your bow tie. I believe that you are very fun. Sincerely, Juniper.

My mom 100% wrote that. I'm not responding.

Juniper would be Jopunopipoper.

My mom is Dopaisopy. Or Mopom.

Lada Hi Mopapople

Hi Lopadopa **Me**

Lada hahaha

hahahahahaha **Me**

Lada hopahopahopahopa

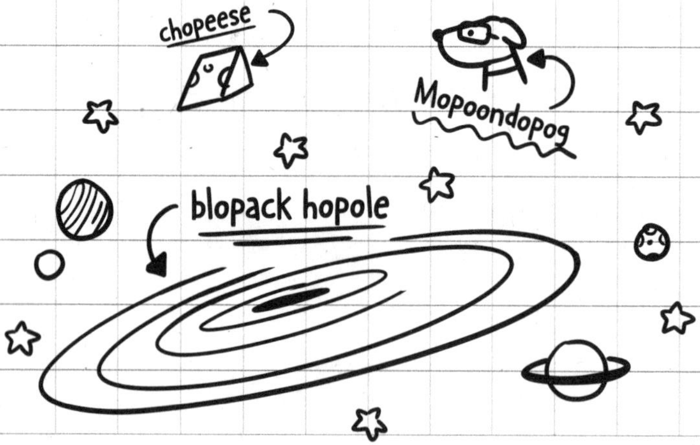

chopeese

Mopoondopog

blopack hopole

We need to stay focused. Lada and I agreed to limit our use of Openglopish to only once a day.

2:04 p.m.

Sunny's name would be Sopunnopy. I bet he'd think that's funny.

Thursday, 4:17 p.m.

Look what we discovered at lunch today:

Shift Cipher

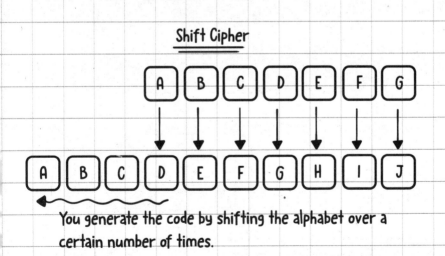

You generate the code by shifting the alphabet over a certain number of times.

Friday, 11:43 a.m.

Lada just had a Nobel Prize-worthy idea. I was adding a temperature setting to my weather app, and it occurred to her that we could use the exact temperature from my app to tell us how many letters to shift the alphabet in our code. That way our code could change every day, just like with the Enigma machine! This is genius.

6:21 p.m.

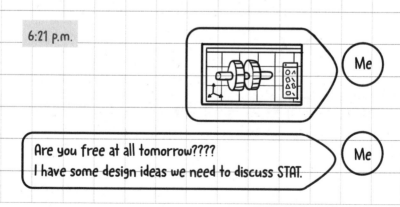

Lada: yes i am free from 7:30 am-9:30 pm

Me: Excellent

Me: [flask] [flask] [laughing face]

Saturday, 9:45 p.m.

Lada was here all day, and I have to say, our final design is AWESOME.

11:03 p.m.

This machine is by far the smartest thing anyone has EVER designed for a 3D printer. Maybe even smarter than the pizza Jackie Grand 3D-printed in space? And WAY more complicated than the laughing bow tie and Sunny's rock display case combined.

IDEA: What if we do a shift cipher but the bottom alphabet is SCRAMBLED?!

wbfhscaio19274b5ncm

4azwsx2dcrfvt9byhnuj7ikolp

nbicmsdfohiklzxcvbnm

The Enigma 2 (TOP SECRET)

Top cylinder = normal alphabet

Bottom cylinder = scrambled alphabet

A	B	C	D	E
Z	W	S	X	2

Rotate bottom cylinder x number of times clockwise

X = daily temperature

Final alignment = code

NOTE: You need BOTH the machine AND the temperature to crack the code

162

Sunday, 1:20 p.m.

In order to print the Enigma 2 in actual plastic, we have to build our design in this special software I have called Sculptibot3D. It's pretty complicated stuff, so I'm not going to have a lot of time to write.

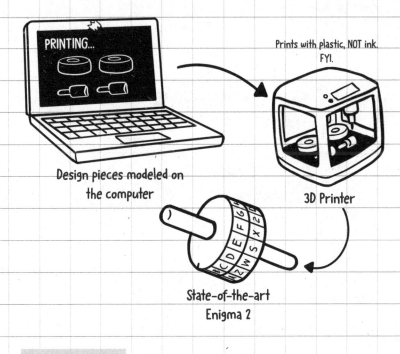

Design pieces modeled on the computer

Prints with plastic, NOT ink. FYI.

3D Printer

State-of-the-art Enigma 2

Monday, 7:43 p.m.

Sculptibot3D keeps crashing. I'm only 12% of the way done.

I saw Sunny in the bus lane again, and we had our BEST CONVERSATION YET about who the villain would be in Moondog 3. He laughed when I suggested that the bad guy could be a flea named Moonflea, and I didn't even use the bow tie!

I think we would have kept talking all the way to science class, but of course Jared came out of nowhere and completely took over the conversation.

Sunny is so much better without Jared Grody.

Hey, Sunny, look! The Bagel Brothers website saved my dad's credit card.

FREE BAGELS FOR LIFE!

In the Maker Lab, Lada asked if she could help more on the Enigma 2, so I showed her how to make a tube in Sculptibot3D. It took me YEARS to get this good at 3D modeling, so I told Lada not to worry if she didn't get the hang of it right away.

Wow, Lada's a natural! She has such good ideas AND she's really helpful in the practical stage. Sunny, Lada, and I are going to be the team to beat FOR SURE. If they want to do it. Which maybe they will?

Our design is DONE!

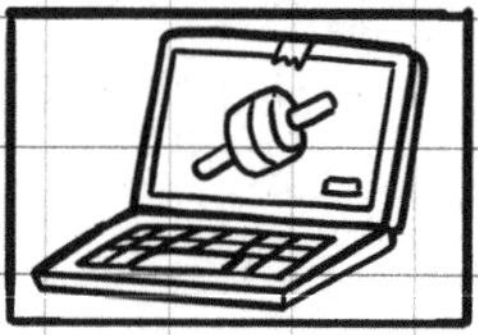

Me

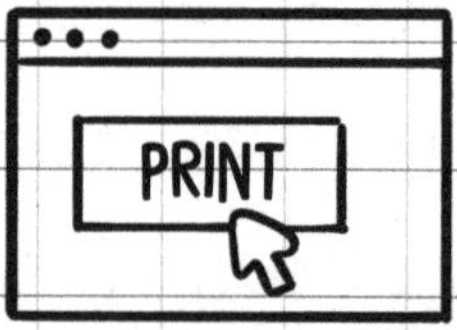

Me

I'm doing it! I'm pressing PRINT!!!! Me

Lada

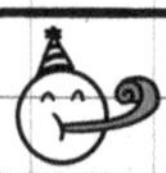

Lada Time to crack the egg for the omelet!

166

I had a dream that an asteroid made of mac and cheese
fell onto our garage and destroyed the Enigma 2. I woke
up really sweaty and ran to check on the print:

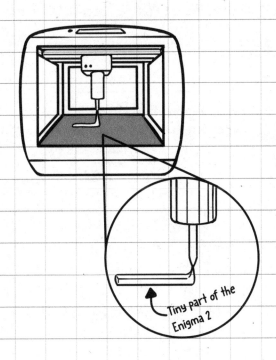

Tiny part of the
Enigma 2

Going perfectly! No cheese anywhere.

Saturday, 10:31 a.m.

Lada came over because we have a full day of printing ahead. We agreed that the Enigma 2 would definitely change the world, probably even more than the first Enigma machine in World War II. Then Lada turned to me and asked:

Maple? You know the Invention Convention that is happening soon?

Oh! Yeah!

Since we're already inventing something that will change the world, I was thinking . . . should we maybe do the Invention Convention together? It's really fun doing this research, and I think we would make a very competitive team. What do you think?

At first, I felt pretty excited. Then I wasn't totally sure what to say because I hadn't even sneakily floated the idea to Sunny yet. But maybe it would be smart to go ahead and get Lada on board now?

I was thinking the same thing!

And maybe there's a third person or something who'd want to join too. I'd definitely be open to that.

Okay, great! A third person is okay with me. Do you know who?

I don't know. I'm just open to it.

Yes, of course. Same here.

Over the Rainbowtie™, let's go!

I'll bring Lada up to speed about Sunny and his qualifications once he agrees to be on our team.

Wow, this is going to be a dream team! We'll be like the ISS astronauts, or those Google guys! Or the Jacuzzi brothers but without the fighting!

11:24 a.m.

Lada showed me one of her rhythmic gymnastics moves while we waited.

11:35 a.m.

We're going to count down the last 800 seconds of the print.

11:46 a.m.

140 seconds left!

11:48 a.m.

94 seconds!

11:48 a.m.

71!

11:53 a.m.

It paused ... still 71 seconds left.

11:58 a.m.

10, 9, 8, 7, 6, 5, 4, 3, 2, 1, IT'S DONE! Time to test it out.

Temperature: 76°
Starting word: eggs

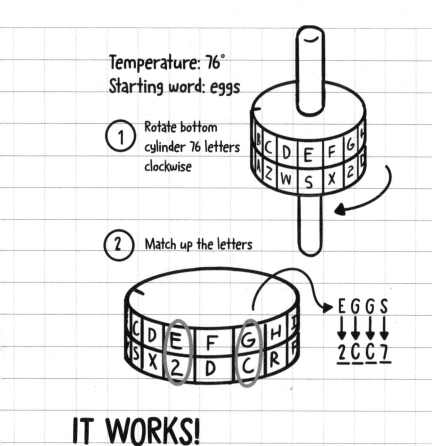

① Rotate bottom cylinder 76 letters clockwise

② Match up the letters

E G G S
↓ ↓ ↓ ↓
2 C C 7

IT WORKS!

12:12 p.m.

Heading to Lada's house to do a more thorough quality-assurance check. I don't trust my family with delicate machinery, especially after the bow-tie fiasco.

QUALITY ASSURANCE CARD		
Subject	Solved Code?	Comments
Uncle Belly	No	He tried to trick us into telling us what the code was with an expired cookie.
Uncle Danish	No	He was busy playing the piano, but said he had "no idea" what 2cc7 meant.
Dr. Katarina	*Incomplete	She asked if we were using a "substitution + shift cipher" for our code. We took it away before she could figure it out.

3:46 p.m.

We practiced writing all kinds of important secret

messages, such as

My name is Lopadopa: B4 yzb2 f7 9hnzxhnz

My name is Mopapople: B4 yzb2 f7·Bhnznhn92

Cheese: sr2272

173

Now that we're SO GOOD at the Enigma 2, Lada suggested that we try using it for its original purpose, which is to open up. I was having such a good time making the Enigma 2 that I completely forgot about the whole horrible, depressing-thoughts part we have to do.

But Lada reminded me that we HAVE to do the unfun part now to have fun later. I agreed to take the Enigma 2 back home to my safe house and do my opening up there.

7:32 p.m.

I was trying to buy a little more time at Lada's house. I really don't want to open up.

174

7:44 p.m.

What did you girls get up to?

Obviously our research.
I told you about it.

Research on a Saturday night?
You know there's a Rocket Grrls
bowling group that meets on
weekends if you're interested.

8:16 p.m.

Juniper has friends over in the backyard.

Can you turn the music down?   Me

Juniper   ▶ ···||||||··· 00:02   (Translation: No)

I can't do my opening up right now.

175

Sunday, 9:33 a.m.

Okay, I guess I'm doing it today.

Maple's Opening Up Message, Attempt

Maple's Opening Up Message, Attempt #5

Maple's Opening Up Message, Attempt #7

Okay. So. I'm pretty sure my mom thinks I'm super unfun. She doesn't understand why I would want to do actual research by myself on a Friday night instead of sparkly, fake science games with people who DON'T EVEN KNOW WHAT THE SCIENTIFIC METHOD IS. My sister definitely thinks I'm unfun, and that every time I get anxious, I just ruin everything around me. And even though my dad is almost never home, I wonder if he requested that high-precision welding job in California instead of Texas because I'm too unfun to even be around? And there are some people at school who have suggested that I'm not very fun as well.

I try to pretend that I don't care, but if I'm being honest,
I think about it ALL THE TIME. Well, not all the time, but
at least three times a day. And every time I think about it,
I become even LESS fun. And then I feel like garbage. That
means I feel like garbage at least THREE TIMES a day.
Sometimes I wonder if I'm actually a human-garbage
hybrid. I just really want the research to work because
I'm kind of tired of feeling like I'm not good enough.

This concludes my opening up.

10:49 a.m.

According to my website, the temperature is exactly 70
degrees, so I shifted the Enigma 2 exactly 70 times.

9zi
^

72
^

o
Kuc2. 4k. H'7 4ptaa2 4zpt 7k7 ayhiu4 H'7 4zotp zi . . .

This is taking forever. I need a protein bar or

something.

Kuc2. 4k. H'7 optaa2 4zpt 72 7k7 ayhiu4 H'7 4zotp zi9zi. 4yt
vkt4i'a zivtp4aciv sy2 H skzjv scia ak vk cfazcj pt4tcpfy r2 724tj9
ki c 9phvc2 ihbya hi4atcv k9 4ocpuj2, 9cut 4fhtift bc7t4 shay
otkojt syk VKI'A TWTI UIKS SYCA AYT 4FHTIAH9HF 7TAYKV H4. 72
4h4atp vt9hihatj2 ayhiu4 H'7 zi9zi, civ ayca twtp2 ah7t H bta
cixhkz4, H nz4a pzhi twtp2ayhib cpkziv 7t. Civ twti aykzby 72 vcv
h4 cj7k4a itwtp yk7t, H skivtp h9 yt ptlzt4atv ayca
yhby-optfh4hki stjvhib nkr hi Fcjh9kpihc hi4atcv k9 Atxc4 rtfcz4t
H'7 akk zi9zi ak twti rt cpkziv? Civ aytpt cpt 4k7t otkojt ca 4fykkj
syk ycwt 4zbbt4atv ayca H'7 ika wtp2 9zi c4 stjj.

H ap2 ak optativ ayca H vki'a fcpt, rza h9 H'7 rthib ykit4a,
H ayhiu crkza ha CJJ AYT AH7T. Stjj, ika cjj ayt ah7t, rza
ca jtc4a ayptt ah7t4 c vc2. Civ twtp2 ah7t H ayhiu crkza ha, H
rtfk7t twti JT44 9zi. Civ ayti H 9ttj jhut bcprcbt. Ayca 7tci4 H 9ttj
jhut bcprcbt ca jtc4a AYPTT AH7T4 c vc2. 4k7tah7t4 H skivtp h9
H'7 cfazcjj2 c yz7ci-bcprcbt y2rphv. H nz4a ptcjj2 scia ayt pt4tcpfy
ak skpu rtfcz4t H'7 uhiv k9 ahptv k9 9ttjhib jhut H'7 ika bkkv
tikzby.

Ayh4 fkifjzvt4 72 kotihib zo.

Finally done! I have to say, the whole opening-up experience wasn't nearly as bad as I thought it would be. I guess I've never actually told anyone about that stuff before. The only way I can think to describe it is that it feels kind of like when you're on a long car ride and you have to pee extremely badly and then you FINALLY do.

Lada was definitely right about doing the unfun thing so you can have fun later. You can't ever have THAT much fun when you really have to pee. Well, now I've peed out all my feelings and I'm READY TO BE FUN.

feelings

Passing my coded message to Lada today! That means I also need to pass her the Enigma 2. Kids can be pretty rowdy with hardware, so I'm going to wrap it in at least four sweaters and some Bubble Wrap.

7:41 a.m.

My mom said she needed her sweater, so I only wrapped it in three. I hope it survives the bus ride.

8:24 a.m.

My attempt to give the package to Lada at the beginning of science was disrupted when Mr. Wormley saw it.

Whatcha got there, Maple?

It's a top secret code machine that Lada and I invented.

180

11:01 a.m.

I guess when I called the Enigma 2 "top secret," that made everyone curious about it. At the beginning of lunch, exactly three people came to my locker asking to try out the machine.

Lada tapped me on the shoulder and warned me that "the mean kid who did the prank call is coming over here," which I realized meant Jared. Then she gave him the hairy eyeball, which looks like this:

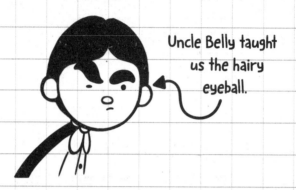

Uncle Belly taught us the hairy eyeball.

Sunny was right behind Jared. I really hope he didn't think the hairy eyeball was for him, when it was clearly for Jared and Jared only. Sunny definitely doesn't deserve a hairy eyeball. He's been EXTREMELY supportive of all our inventions lately.

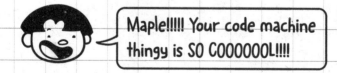

Maple!!!!! Your code machine thingy is SO COOOOOOL!!!!

Face = 42% red

Cool and also highly effective!

How does it work? Can I try it? Can you encode a top secret message, please? Please, please, please? I'll whisper it. It's "butt."

I didn't know what to say because I obviously wanted Sunny to be excited about our work, but my opening-up message was RIGHT THERE in my backpack, and I wanted to make sure it was 100% IMPOSSIBLE for him to EVER read it.

Top secret means top secret. Nobody can know the code but us. We will not encode "butt."

Then Jared kind of took over even though it didn't concern him AT ALL, and he started chanting:

I could feel myself turning even redder, and I really wanted them to stop cheering. I pulled Lada aside and asked if we should consider reconsidering, since this seemed like a potential opportunity to show how far we'd come in our fun research. Lada strongly disagreed and said, "Absolutely not."

Face = 98% red

After everyone left, Lada went on and on about how much she hates when people say "do it, do it" to make someone do something they don't want to do. I pretty much agreed, although sometimes I think disappointing people feels even worse. I just wish she could've told everyone to leave in a nicer way.

11:30 a.m.

Lada is currently decoding my message in the Maker Lab. I decided to text Sunny just so he knew we weren't mad or anything.

> This is Maple, I think this is your new number. — Me

> I can show you the Enigma 2 as soon as we finish our beta testing, don't worry. — Me

> Sorry about what Lada said, she's just really committed to scientific discovery. — Me

> Thank you for your patience. — Me

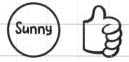

I think that went really well.

4:08 p.m.

After school, Sunny texted me a completely unrelated message that wasn't in response to anything!

MOONDOG PEES ON FIRE, SAVES TOWN

8:29 p.m.

I wanted to find the perfect hilarious clip to send back, so I spent three hours watching Moondog 2 and then

<u>Moondog 1.</u> Nada. Which means that I didn't find anything. But then I remembered that dog crowd-surfing video that got three HAs from Lada, so I sent that over to Sunny.

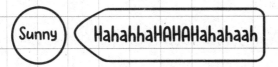

Sunny: HahahhaHAHAHahahaah

I knew it: he and Lada 100% have the same sense of humor! I wonder if I should ask him to be on our team soon. . . .

<u>No way.</u> Lada and I still have to do something scary. And asking him actually sounds terrifying.

Wait.

Scientific breakthrough.

Asking Sunny to join our team = DOING SOMETHING SCARY. This is it! I can do something scary and complete all four elements of fun JUST in time for Sunny to say yes!

Maybe I should text him RIGHT NOW. No. That would be too easy. Texting is only 30% scary, and I should probably pick the scariest available option. I should ask him IRL. Which means IN REAL LIFE.

10:16 p.m.

I came up with the perfect speech and practiced it in front of the mirror. It goes like this:

11:01 p.m.

The three of us are going to make possibly the best team ever, so all of this is totally worth it. I wonder what we should name our planet when we win?

IDEAS:

1. Maple, Sunny, and Lada's planet

11:34 p.m.

Okay, going to sleep so I can be physically and mentally prepared to ask my extremely scary question tomorrow. 100% fun, HERE I COME!!!

Lada came into science 12 minutes late, and she looked horrible.

She said it took her all day and night to decode my opening up and encode her response, which she had safely sealed in a TRIPLE envelope for extra security. We did a secret handoff under the desk, and I tucked it very carefully into my backpack.

Lada passed me another note.

~~Relax~~

~~Have a sense of humor~~

~~Open up~~

Do something scary

...We finished #3, right?

I nodded, and at the same time I could
feel my hands start to get a little sweaty.
I probably should've mentioned the whole
asking-Sunny thing to Lada; then at
least I could ask to borrow her Relaxium
for what I'm about to do. I'll explain
everything really soon.

Sweat stain →

Hey, Sunny. Want to be on a team with me and Lada for the Invention Convention?

Hey, Sunny. Want to be on a team with me and Lada for the Invention Convention?

Hey, Sunny. Want to be on a team with me and Lada for the Invention Convention?

9:07 a.m.

I walked by Sunny's locker after science, but he was busy talking to Jared and Titus. Okay, I'll do it later. No big deal. Just staying relaxed.

9:54 a.m.

Ugh, they're there again! Maybe I should just do the scary thing another day. Or maybe never. Do I actually NEED to be 100% fun? Maybe 75% is enough?

9:58 a.m.

But if I want Sunny to join my team . . . I have to ask him at some point. There's no way around it. This is TOO IMPORTANT. For the sake of our pact . . . and our entire 7.2 years of friendship . . . and our 80 to 100 years of future friendship (also with Lada) . . . I'm going to do it today.

2:01 p.m.

Sunny is going to his locker. THIS IS THE MOMENT.

I'm squishing the Relaxium <u>**REALLY HARD.**</u>

I'M GOING IN.

4:02 p.m.

Update: there's been a little bit of a change in plans.

I squished the Relaxium twice, went to Sunny's locker, and said my lines PERFECTLY. Well, I stuttered a little bit, but the main point definitely came across.

Hey, Sunny. Want to be on a team with me and Lada for the Invention Convention? You know, since we had a pact for it and everything, would you still want to do it with me?

Oh, yaaaa! Wait, let me check. I told Jared and Titus that we'd do a K-Rap song together, but we still need a fourth person for our final dance since Kelvin Juma broke his femur.

What's K-Rap?

Then Sunny shouted across the hall to Jared and Titus, who I didn't even KNOW were there, and asked if I could join.

Okay, so K-Rap is this whole new genre of music we invented that's going to COMPLETELY change our cultural landscape. It's karate WHILE rapping. And Mr. Wormley said it counted!

C'mooooooooon, Maple! You PROMISED to do the Invention Convention with me a billion years ago!!!! We had a pact, remember? You HAAAAVE to say yes!

So basically, I had to choose between keeping my promise to Sunny and keeping my promise to Lada. I WANTED to say something like "K-Rap is NOT a real invention and Jared is below average in every way including both smartness and niceness and you should join ME AND LADA instead." But, OF COURSE, the words didn't want to come out. And everybody was staring at me. And Sunny REALLY wanted me to say yes.

196

Come on, Maple, pleeeeeease????
Ma-ple! Ma-ple!

Ma-ple! Ma-ple! Ma-ple!

I felt myself go 101% red. I know that's technically impossible but that's what it felt like. I DIDN'T KNOW WHAT TO DO. So, in the heat of the moment, I said, "Okay."

WOOOOOOOOO!!

I felt pretty queasy walking to the bus lane after that. Technically Sunny is right that I promised I would do the Invention Convention with him WAY before I even met Lada. But I also promised Lada I would do it with her. But I promised Sunny first, which technically cancels out the promise I made to Lada. So technically I'm doing the right thing.

Right?

4:33 p.m.

Lada just texted me a bunch of ideas about doing something scary for our fun research.

Lada — We could fly a plane ourselves with no training at all!

Lada — We could eat puffer fish! Very poisonous and we might die right away!

Lada

This weekend we could watch all of the scary movies that I found on a list titled "Movies that will make you wish you were never born."

I have no idea what to say. I'm going to turn my phone off for the rest of the bus ride and pretend it ran out of battery.

6:58 p.m.

What should I say to Lada?

how do I tell my friend that I'm not doing the Invention Convention with her anymore because I promised my other friend I would do it first?

how do you break a promise?

why am i so sweaty 🔍

am i having a heart attack 🔍

can you die from being anxious 🔍

can you die from your friend being mad at you 🔍

can you go to jail from your friend being mad at you ⁉️?

8:09 p.m.

Lada just texted me "hello?" I think I need to do this now.

Here's what I'm going to say:

200

~~Good evening~~ ~~Sup Lada~~ ~~How's it going?~~

~~Hey Lada~~ ~~Hi Lada~~ ~~Heyyyy~~ ～～～～～～～～

I am very sorry to report that I made an error when I said I could do the Invention Convention with you. I promised Sunny I would do it with him 3.5 years ago. I am very sorry for the confusion. I think Mahogany Perez is looking for a partner and she's probably the smartest person at our school so you guys will probably win. I hope you're not mad. I'm still decoding your letter. Maple.

Me

I should probably send it from the bathroom because it's closer to the Wi-Fi router.

8:40 p.m.

I still haven't sent it. If I don't send it now, then I'm going to have to tell her in person, and I would rather go on a thousand bouncy houses than do that.

Maybe some Relaxium will help. I'm squeezing it.

1

2

3

3.5555555555

Sent.

I'm turning my phone off and going to sleep. Good
night.

Unless you do the Invention
Convention with your old
friend even though you also
had a promise to do it with
your new one.

A friendship never sinks.

Just turned on my phone to check my texts. Nada.
Maybe Lada took a surprise vacation and didn't even
get my—

Oh. She responded.

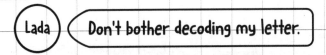

Oh no.

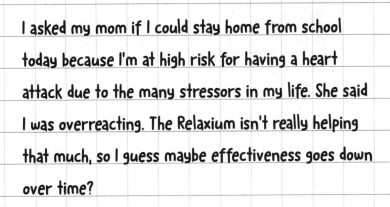

I asked my mom if I could stay home from school
today because I'm at high risk for having a heart
attack due to the many stressors in my life. She said
I was overreacting. The Relaxium isn't really helping
that much, so I guess maybe effectiveness goes down
over time?

203

Lada hasn't come into science yet. Maybe she's so mad, she took a surprise vacation after all?

Never mind. Lada came in just as the bell was about to ring. She didn't look at me at all or say hi. She's REALLY mad.

Eyebrows pointed DOWN

No eye contact

Body positioned away from me even though definitely more comfortable to face forward

I tried to say something to Lada after class, but she got up and left within seconds. I'm going to try again in Spanish class.

No success. Lada moved seats and sat all the way across the room. I tried passing her a note in Openglopish, but then she went to the bathroom for twenty-two minutes and I saw her throw the note out in the hallway trash. I have no idea what to do. I was thinking I could reprogram the bow tie to say "I'm sorry" but my bow-tie recorder is **STILL BROKEN**.

I had a whole plan to go to the track at lunch to talk to her, but Jared, Sunny, and Titus ambushed me in the hall. Apparently, I had to get "onboarded" ASAP if we wanted to learn the routine in time, so I'm going to have to spend every lunch rehearsing with them in the dance studio. I didn't even know our school HAD a dance studio.

They made me watch the routine on YouTube on the way so I could be "caught up on the moves." So, they BARELY even invented this dance.

EXTREME HIP-HOP KARATE DANCE ROUTINE

Jared told us the agenda, and it started with two minutes of screaming and head-banging to "get into the zone." This is definitely how you get a traumatic brain injury and also rip your voice box. Then we practiced some fighting formations and I learned a little bit of the rap, which went like this:

For Maple

K-RAP!
Attack, attack!

Give 'em a kick
and also a SMACK!

Nobody screw
with the K-Rap crew!

If you do,
we'll ANNIHILATE you!

It's kind of violent, but Jared said "that's the point."

We have a really strict schedule for the weekend, too.

K-RAP SCHEDULE	
Saturday:	Sunday:
• 9 a.m. - 11 a.m. Photo shoot	• 9 a.m. - 12 p.m. Surprise a Make-A-Wish kid
• 11 a.m. - 2 p.m. Music video taping	(Does anyone know any Make-A-Wish kids?)
• 3 p.m. - 7 p.m. Sign posters at Jared's	• 1 p.m. - 7 p.m. PRACTICE!
• 7 p.m. - 1 a.m. PRACTICE!	

We're not allowed to miss even one minute of it or we could be kicked off the team.

Thursday, 11:22 a.m.

Lada didn't talk to me today either. Oh, and at K-Rap practice, I saw Jared use his T-shirt as a tissue. I can't stop thinking about it.

Sunny forgot to reserve the dance studio today, so now we have to practice at Jared's house after school. I told everyone that my mom probably couldn't drive me due to her very busy job at NASA, but Sunny said I could carpool with him. Ugh. I guess I'm going to Jared's house.

4:07 p.m.

I haven't been in Mr. Gwon's car for a really long time, and it still smells like how I remember (kind of like Fruit Roll-Ups). He said it was nice to see me in real life and not on the phone. Sunny told Mr. Gwon all about my bow tie and the Enigma 2 and how I was completely saving the whole team and it's going to be soooooooo fun.

It felt a little like old times, especially when Sunny and I started talking about merch we could make for Moondog 3, like a dog bone that gives you mind-control powers. For a second, I actually felt okay because

Sunny was being so nice to me and I guess I kind of missed that.

But then I saw Lada get into Uncle Belly's car, and she didn't wave back when I waved. I didn't really say anything for the rest of the car ride.

4:18 p.m.

Jared's house is not like I expected at all.

210

I think if I told my parents to make me Pop-Tarts and evacuate the premises, they would take away my 3D-printing privileges forever.

Everyone was kind of talking and joking around, so I told Sunny that we should use our Moondog bones to mind-control OUR parents into bringing us snacks. Sunny started to say something, but of course Jared jumped in and said:

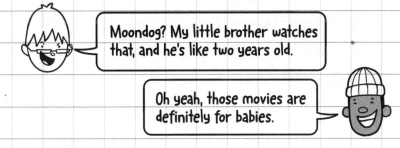

Moondog? My little brother watches that, and he's like two years old.

Oh yeah, those movies are definitely for babies.

I looked at Sunny for backup, but all he said was this:

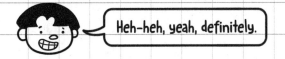

Heh-heh, yeah, definitely.

I felt my face go right back to 99% red. I can't believe Sunny didn't say ANYTHING to defend Moondog. WE'RE not babies, and WE saw the first Moondog eight times. I just don't understand why Sunny would go along with them like that.

After that, I started to feel unsure about what was okay to talk about.

Ideas for Conversation:

−Obviously not Moondog.

−That probably counts out the moon too.

−And also dogs.

−And probably a lot of other conversation topics that I thought were fun but turned out to be not fun at all.

Jared started complaining about how annoying his parents are (even though they do everything he says). I just kept saying "be fun, be fun, be fun" in my mind, but I don't even know what that means in this situation. I couldn't think of ANYTHING to add to the conversation. I wish I had my bow tie.

I heard Sunny say, "Where's Maple?" so I guess I have to come out of the bathroom soon. I've probably been hiding out in here for a little too long.

Ugh, there's a part of the routine where we all say our "K-Rap names." Sunny is "Suns-out-guns-out" and Jared is "J-RAD." Titus Jemison is "Mightus Titus." I obviously didn't have one, so Jared made one up for me.

MAPE.

It's by far the worst name, but I can't think of anything better. I have to rap "I'm Mape" and strike one of three possible poses that Jared assigned to me:

I think this one is the least embarrassing?

1. 2. 3.

I really hope we don't get that far in our practice today.

As a warm-up, Jared made us karate-kick dried spaghetti while screaming, "Come on, spaghetti, show me whatcha got. I got a foot that's hotter than hot." I think it's some chant he learned at camp, because I don't think Jared's clever enough to come up with that rhyme on his own.

I couldn't really get my vocal cords to cooperate, so I decided to just mouth the words. Jared didn't let that slide, though.

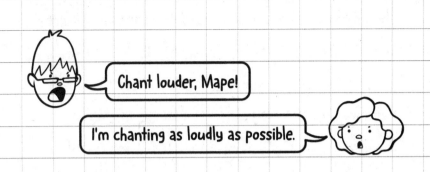

Chant louder, Mape!

I'm chanting as loudly as possible.

He told the other boys to stop shouting so he could listen to my technique, which made me immediately panic. I looked at Sunny, but all he said was, "I KNOW you can be suuuuuuper loud, Maple," so I closed my eyes and yelled the stupid thing. Well, what came out was more like a horrible wheezy whisper than a yell.

Come on, spaghetti, show me whatcha got. I got a foot that's hotter than hot.

Then we started practicing the "freestyle rap" portion, where we're supposed to actually MAKE UP the rap as we go. I decided to head back to the bathroom (where I am now), and I don't plan on leaving for at least 30 minutes. Or maybe only 15 minutes? I don't want everyone to think I have diarrhea.

Oh no, I hear someone saying, "Mape, we need you." Maybe if I don't say anything . . . Never mind. Sunny is knocking on the bathroom door. I told Sunny I need ONE SECOND. I don't want to go back out there.

I guess one second is up. Not that Sunny even cares about being accurate with timing. He's still knocking, so I'd better go back out there.

Ugh.

Wish me luck.

Update: there's been another change in plans.

I came out of the bathroom, and everybody was working on the final dance sequence where the whole team huddles and throws one member up in the air. The flying person is supposed to do a kick while shouting "K-RAP SLAPS" from up in the air. Since I'm the smallest, I HAD to be the flyer.

I didn't want to hit my head on the ceiling, but Jared insisted that Titus and Sunny were way too weak to throw me that high. I wasn't convinced they could even catch me when I came back down, but Sunny stepped in and said they did it looooaaaaaads of times with Kelvin and they didn't drop anyone. Yet. How exactly did Kelvin Juma break his femur again?

 I know you can do it! Pleeeeeaaaaase.

217

I didn't want to let an entire team down, so I said, "Fine."

They huddled in a circle, and I started to climb up onto their hands, but it was so wobbly that I immediately had to step off. I didn't have my phone with me to confirm, but I was pretty positive that cheerleaders and stunt people die ALL THE TIME doing dangerous stuff like this.

Jared yelled at Titus for not bracing his forearms, and I tried again. It was STILL too wobbly, so I got off. Jared glared at Sunny, which made Sunny start cheering, "Do it, do it, do it!" even as I was backing away.

I felt kind of embarrassed that I couldn't just get on like they wanted me to. But it wasn't that I was too scared to do it. It was just TOO WOBBLY.

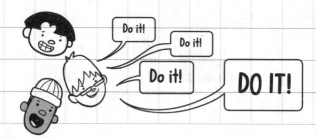

Then I started to feel a little frustrated that Sunny would chant "do it, do it" when it was an obvious SAFETY HAZARD and I obviously didn't want to do it. Did he WANT me to smash my head into the ceiling? Was he just saying that so Jared wouldn't get mad? Honestly, that felt extremely irresponsible. And not something at ALL that a good friend would do.

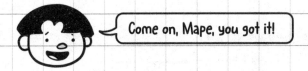

Come on, Mape, you got it!

Then I started to feel kind of mad.

I told Sunny that I HATE it when people say "do it, do it." And Lada hates it too. She would never in a million years make me do something UNSAFE after I said no three times.

Sunny turned kind of red and said, "Sorry, sorry, sorry" and "You're right, you're right, you're right."

I thought maybe I had gotten my point across . . .

. . . until he went on and said it was reeeaaaaally important for me to do just this one thing and then he would never ever, ever, ever ask for anything ever again. And I didn't even have to rap in the group part if I didn't want to!

That was the last straw.

You're not LISTENING to me! You actually NEVER listen to me! You do this ALL THE TIME.

You did it with the Enigma 2 when we didn't want to encode the word "butt." You did it when I didn't have a good answer in your Velociraptor-Roomba debate. And you did it when I didn't want to go on the bouncy house, and THEN I MISSED MEETING JACKIE GRAND! You don't listen to me AT ALL, and honestly, that makes you a BAD FRIEND.

Lada was probably the best friend I've ever had, and letting her down for this stupid team was the WORST mistake I've made in my eleven years. So, YOU KNOW WHAT?

I walked out and locked myself in the bathroom. I
texted my mom:

It's an emergency.   Me

Please come get me STAT.

She's on her way now.

5:29 p.m.

My mom keeps asking what the emergency was, but I'm
WAY too upset to talk to anyone right now.

I really messed EVERYTHING up. I should never in a million years have chosen Sunny over Lada. I wish I could text her and tell her everything, but she definitely doesn't want to hear from me.

5:39 p.m.

ARGHHHH WHAT A HUGE MISTAKE.

5:42 p.m.

I know Lada said not to bother decoding her letter, but I'm going to anyway.

222

Lada's Opening Up Letter.
71 degrees.

Dearest Maple,

Long ago (5 months, specifically), I was very afraid to move to the United States of America (USA). I told my mom on the first day of school that the children here didn't like me very much, or my ponytail (far too long), or my sweater with the many practical pockets (far too many pockets). I told her that I would like to request a ticket back to Hungary at first daylight, and that I was even prepared to journey by myself. I missed my old dance teacher and my old friends and all the smells in my old house (such as almonds, chocolate, dust, oak, elm, cat hair, and fried bread, which I think you would enjoy, Maple, but only in small quantities (very unhealthy)).

One fateful Saturday, I was planning to stay home and finish <u>The Apothecary's Daughter: Infectious Smiles</u>, when my mom told me about an ice cream workshop at her place of work. I am glad I went because <u>Infectious Smiles</u> was poorly written . . . and because the workshop is where WE BECAME FRIENDS. I love doing research with you, but if I am being honest, it is only 33.333% for the research. The other 66.666% is because I just like doing things together. We could be researching toe hair and I would still have fun. I cannot wait to do the Invention Convention together and then many other things.

Lada.

P.S. Anybody who thinks you are not fun should come to me, and I will set the record straight (with force, if I must). Also, I would still want to be friends even if you were a human-garbage hybrid.

Well, at least now I know I'm not a human-garbage hybrid. I'm 100% garbage.

Before, I felt REALLY angry, but now I just feel awful. Like how Jackie Grand would PROBABLY feel if she steered her space shuttle right into a crater and broke the air lock and her whole crew got sucked up into space. But of course, she would never do that.

I really, really, really messed up.

I'm going to stay in bed all day. There's no point in getting up when my best friend hates me.

10:11 a.m.

Update: My mom made me get up so she can vacuum my bunker. I didn't even have the energy to tell her not to bother.

10:28 a.m.

Why is my mom shouting my name? Why can't everyone just leave me alone for the next 80 to 100 years?

Oh, it's about the "blue goo" that is clogging the vacuum cleaner. That was supposed to be my new batch of Relaxium. I wish my mom and Juniper and everyone I ever knew would just

GO AWAY.

Correction: I take back that thing I said about my mom.

I went to my room to deal with the Relaxium, but the second I saw it, some dust must have exploded into my eyes or something, because I suddenly felt so horrible that all I could do was bury my head in my pillow and let my tear ducts flush out all the dust. With tears.

My mom asked me what was wrong, so I finally told her that the "blue goo" was the Relaxium I made with Lada as part of our fun research. And she should DEFINITELY not throw any of it away, not even one drop.

My tear ducts kind of went into overdrive right then, which has NEVER happened before. Except maybe that time I watched that movie about the dog with two legs.

Flippy's Final Hour

Do NOT watch this movie.

I told my mom that even though I technically succeeded . . . and figured out how to be fun . . . and got Sunny back after he ditched me at the Fun Fair . . . NONE of it was worth it because I lost Lada. I never had to worry about impressing Lada, because she already liked to do all the scientific things I liked to do! And now she hates me, and it's probably the worst thing I've ever felt. Worse than that time I got stung by six bees.

My mom came over and gave me a really big hug, which helped about 1 or maybe 2%. She asked why I didn't tell her about what was going on with my friends.

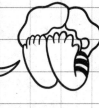

Because even YOU think I'm unfun. I don't like sparkles and googly eyes. And I hate spelling the word "girls" as "grrls." You think my research is pointless, and that I can never be fun.

I'm so sorry, Maple. I had no idea.

You don't have to like sparkles and googly eyes! Or lunar-eclipse parties!

OR Rocket Grrls bowling nights.

All I want is for you to go out there and make friends and participate in things you love. I'm sorry I made you feel like you aren't good enough exactly as you are.

Yeah.

Lada never made me feel like that. Even though I'm a below-average friend who breaks promises, who doesn't speak up when I need to, and who can't even be fun without a serious scientific intervention.

I thought my mom would agree with me completely, but she said good science is all about second chances.

Think about how many chances it took for NASA to get an astronaut on the moon. It wasn't until Apollo 11!

I guess that's sort of true. . . .

You would give ME a second chance, right? I'm sure Lada will do the same.

Then she hugged me really tightly, which made me feel a whole 10 to 15% better. She added that she "wasn't eavesdropping or anything," but she overheard a little bit of what Lada and I were working on, and based on "all the evidence," she thought we were BOTH having lots of fun.

One of the things I love most about you is that you ALWAYS figure out a solution. I bet you can dig deep into that scientific brain of yours and find a way to make things right with Lada.

It felt nice to hear her say that, even though it'll be almost impossible to come up with any good ideas by myself.

My mom wiped the Relaxium off the vacuum and gave it back to me. She said she should get me to teach a Relaxium workshop at NASA one of these days. I'll consider it, but she'd have to pay me.

1:20 p.m.

I guess opening up still works, because I feel less like garbage and more like a human since talking to my mom.

1:23 p.m.

I just wish I could think of SOME way to make things right with Lada.

IDEAS:

- Nothing.

I tried doing a headstand to get more blood flowing to my brain, but it ended up sending more tears to my eyes.

I hear a lot of tense whispering from downstairs. My mom is probably calling everyone to tell them that I've permanently transformed into Mople and they should stay away for their own protection.

1:56 p.m.

I guarantee you won't be able to guess who knocked on my door:

JUNIPER.

I don't think she's ever knocked in her entire 16 smelly years of existence.

I completely forgot about Moondog 3. I told her I didn't have anyone to go with and I'm too young to go alone (legally). Then Juniper did something TRULY shocking. She took $10 out of her pocket and waved it in front of me.

We?

So now I'm going to <u>Moondog 3</u> . . . with Juniper. I thought maybe it was some kind of awful prank, but we're pulling up to the movie theater right now. My mom even let Juniper borrow the car! I know I should go back home and think about ways to make it up to Lada, but a super-quick movie break probably won't hurt.

4:50 p.m.

<u>Moondog 3</u> was great, and DEFINITELY NOT FOR BABIES like Jared falsely claimed. Juniper thought it was unrealistic for a dog to be elected mayor of the colony on the moon, and I generally agreed with her. But other than that, pretty great.

There was also this one point in the movie, where Moondog is about to quit the election, that gave me a good idea.

The music gets super sad, but then Moondog goes home and finds a care package that his mom, Momdog, sent all the way from Earth. And it's full of all his favorite dog treats and dog toys and even a little bit of dirt from his favorite park from when he was a puppy.

1:04

1:08

Then the music gets really dramatic, and Moondog decides to go back and finish what he started.

AND HE WINS THE ELECTION!
The care package really turns everything around for Moondog.

1:16

1:32

Final dance number (maybe a little silly).

236

Here's what I'm thinking: I should make Lada a care package full of Lada treats.

I'm going to make a list of ALL her favorite things, put them in a basket, and deliver the basket to her house tomorrow morning, and then maybe possibly she will think about forgiving me and taking me back as a friend/co-scientist/co-inventor. But if she doesn't, I will understand and just be sad forever. Juniper thought this was a good idea too, for the record.

8:15 p.m.

THE "I'M SORRY, LADA" KIT

Homemade cheese-bunny ice cream soup

Cut-up curtains

New rhythmic gymnastics ribbons

Sticks from yard

I'M SORRY!

I'm Sorry Bow Tie (just the laughter bow tie, but reprogrammed to say "I'm sorry")

Lada's OWN Sculptibot3D account!
Username: aLADAgoodideas

A picture from
The Apothecary's Daughter:
Death by Daybreak, printed for
Lada's locker

Wart cream

10:33 p.m.

The "I'm Sorry, Lada" Kit is starting to shape up, I have to
say.

My mom helped me make the cheese-bunny ice cream
soup after dinner, and it turned out pretty decent.
Juniper helped me make ribbons out of the curtains
we used to have in the living room, which we decided
not to tell my mom about. And after maybe forty-five
minutes of trying to fix the recorder, I just put in new
batteries and it worked fine. Huh.

238

OFFICIAL
"I'M SORRY, LADA" KIT
FROM: MAPLE MCNUTT

My mom added these googly
eyes and the glitter. I guess I
can leave them on for now.

11:06 p.m.

"I'm Sorry, Lada" Kit: complete. Map to Lada's house:
printed. Estimated arrival time: sunrise.

My mom said she could drive me tomorrow morning
to drop it off, but I think this is something I need to
do by myself. I just hope Lada forgives me. I'm going
to get a good night's sleep. I'll need 100% of my energy
tomorrow!

According to my weather website, it's raining. Also according to my eyes and ears. Maybe I should reschedule my trip to Lada's house?

No, I'm NOT rescheduling my trip. It's too important. But I AM going to bring my

umbrella hat and reflectors and pack my raft in my backpack in case there's a flash flood.

I told my mom that she had permission to track my phone and reminded her that I have a birthmark next to my left armpit if she needs to identify me in the hospital.

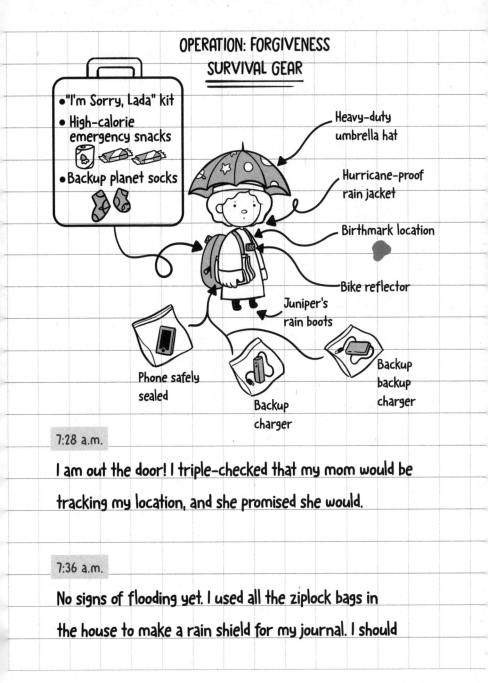

OPERATION: FORGIVENESS
SURVIVAL GEAR

- "I'm Sorry, Lada" kit
- High-calorie emergency snacks
- Backup planet socks

Heavy-duty umbrella hat

Hurricane-proof rain jacket

Birthmark location

Bike reflector

Juniper's rain boots

Phone safely sealed

Backup charger

Backup backup charger

7:28 a.m.

I am out the door! I triple-checked that my mom would be tracking my location, and she promised she would.

7:36 a.m.

No signs of flooding yet. I used all the ziplock bags in the house to make a rain shield for my journal. I should probably stop writing, though. I need to be hyperalert in case any cars veer off the road.

7:43 a.m.

Wow, being hyperalert really makes you notice things you don't usually see. There's a house two streets down from me that's completely purple. I had no idea!

7:49 a.m.

I saw a squirrel! I didn't know there was so much wildlife around here. Maybe I'll do this more often, like once a week. Or month. Maybe just once a year. Ideally not when it's raining.

7:51 a.m.

The rain is clearing up, and I can see Lada's house. I'm just going to stop for a quick snack to keep my energy at peak levels.

7:57 a.m.

I probably don't need to wear my umbrella hat and reflectors all the way up to the door, so I'm dropping them off by the huge tree in front of Lada's house.

8:01 a.m.

I'm just going to draw a few relaxation spirals.

8:05 a.m.

Okay, I'm at Lada's door! Ringing the doorbell in approximately ten seconds. Actually, maybe in two minutes, so I can get in the zone.

8:06 a.m.

Somebody is playing music inside, so I should probably wait until they're done. I KNOW I'm procrastinating, but I'm nervous!!!!!

8:07 a.m.

I squeezed my Relaxium and rang the bell!

8:15 a.m.

Dr. Katarina came to the door. I said exactly what I planned, which was "Hi, is Lada here? I need to deliver an extremely important package." Dr. Katarina said, "Hello,

hello!" and that Lada was upstairs. I couldn't tell if she knew what was going on, but it didn't seem like she hated me, so maybe not?

Dr. Katarina shouted up to Lada in Hungarian, and Lada yelled something back down. Then Dr. Katarina said I could just leave the package and she would make sure Lada got it. I wasn't sure what to do, so I just said "okay" and left.

8:23 a.m.

Phew, no one stole my unattended umbrella hat and reflectors. I can't tell if that went well or not. Dr. Katarina is a woman of her word, though, so if she said that Lada would get the package, then I believe her.

Uh-oh. Lada is looking out her window, and she can definitely see me. I gotta go!

A Journal, Lost: Chapter 1

A very big conundrum. To read or not to read . . .
this journal that was left mysteriously by the tree in
front of my house along with some granola crumbs
and an almost-empty Muscleman protein beverage
bottle, flavor strawberry.

On the left hand, it would be wrong to read
another's diary. On the right hand, the "another"
in question has WRONGED ME GREATLY, for she
has both broken a sacred vow (to do the Invention
Convention with me) and has treated me like a
wooden training sword, cast aside when the battle
comes (which is a simile for the way I have been
treated like a backup friend).

Will our heroine, whose name happens to be Lada, read the mysterious secret journal? Does she forgive the one who wronged her?

Is there going to be a duel TO THE DEATH?

OBVIOUSLY YOU WILL HAVE TO WAIT UNTIL THE NEXT CHAPTER TO FIND OUT!!!!

Lada

A Journal, Lost: Chapter 2

I could not resist. I read it.

Maple here. I guess I accidentally dropped my journal by that tree in front of Lada's house. Because she found it . . . and read the WHOLE THING.

She came to my house in the afternoon with my journal. At first, I was extremely concerned about the fact that Lada had definitely read my early comments about her ponytail, but in my defense, I was just quoting facts for the most part.

She said that even though I hurt her feelings a lot when I broke my promise and treated her like a backup second-place friend, she could tell that I was really sorry and that I cared about our friendship "as deeply as the Mariana Trench" (TRUE and TRUE). And also, she really liked how I gave it to the K-Rap team because they definitely deserved it.

250

And then, most important update in this whole journal:

We ate some of the leftover cheese-bunny ice cream soup in the kitchen—I'd made at least three batches before getting the one for Lada's "I'm Sorry" kit just right.

LADA FORGAVE ME. I can't believe she forgave me. I'm 50% relieved and 50% EXCITED and another 50% relieved. Don't bother me about my math.

8:01 p.m.

I texted Lada IAGTWAF three more times because I just felt like she needed to know.

I went to Lada's locker, and she had hung up ALL the pictures I printed of characters from the Apothecary's Daughter.

9:16 a.m.

Lada isn't mad anymore!!!!!!

2:16 p.m.

Mr. Wormley let me and Lada sign up together even though it's after the team sign-up deadline. Only one week until we have to turn in our idea for the Invention

Life is tough.
YOU are tougher.

Maybe this is . . .
actually kind of true?

Convention! Lada and I are definitely going to need to put in some extra hours of brainstorming to figure out our idea. Lada invited me to her house on Friday for a sleepover, "like they do in American movies."

3:42 p.m.

I saw Sunny looking at me during computer science, but I'm not going to let him distract me anymore. I even turned off my phone, which I've only done twice since I got it!

3:51 p.m.

Turning it back on in case of an emergency.

5:24 p.m.

I asked my mom if I could stay at Lada's Friday night to brainstorm, and she said, "Of course! Have fun with your research." She didn't even mention the Rocket Grrls bowling group.

Going to school is so much better now that Lada isn't mad at me.

11:45 a.m.

We started brainstorming potential ideas in the Maker Lab, but we didn't come up with much. Mahogany Perez was already working on hers in the corner! We've got to get moving!

255

Lada texted me some more ideas.

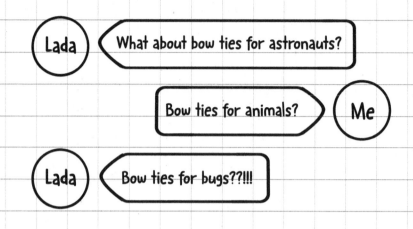

Lada — What about bow ties for astronauts?

Bow ties for animals? — Me

Lada — Bow ties for bugs??!!!

7:25 p.m.

I should probably start packing now for my sleepover at Lada's, since it's only two days away. Her uncles play a lot of instruments, so maybe I should pack my earplugs? I looked up Lada's house, and apparently it isn't in a floodplain. Still, you can never be too sure these days, so I'm also packing my emergency raft. Also my eco-straw.

> Immediately sanitizes water, in case all the pipes burst and we have to drink out of puddles.

256

How about a Relaxium bed?

Or a Relaxium house????

I don't know, is that structurally sound?

3:53 p.m.

Lada said that Uncle Belly downloaded three movies for us in case we need to take a break from brainstorming during the night. I think it's unlikely that we'll have time, but it's nice of him to do that.

Friday, 8:42 a.m.

Today is the day! I just remembered that I didn't pack my fire extinguisher.

9:21 a.m.

Lada said that her house has a fire extinguisher, so it's okay.

11:12 a.m.

4:08 p.m.

Uncle Belly picked us up after school. I texted my mom that it would be much more efficient for me to be picked up from school instead of taking the bus in the future, but she didn't respond.

Brainstorm time!

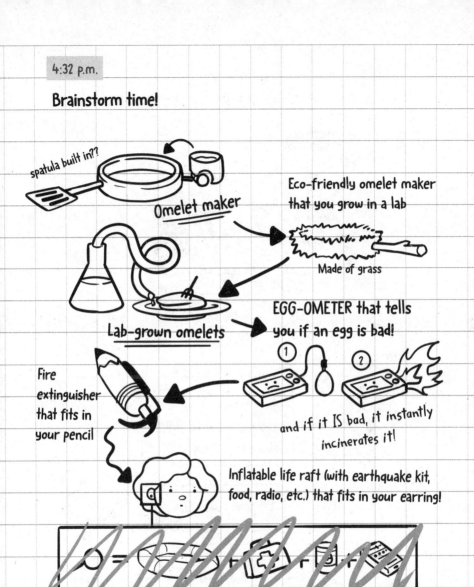

spatula built in??

Omelet maker

Eco-friendly omelet maker that you grow in a lab

Made of grass

Lab-grown omelets

EGG-OMETER that tells you if an egg is bad!

① ②

Fire extinguisher that fits in your pencil

and if it IS bad, it instantly incinerates it!

Inflatable life raft (with earthquake kit, food, radio, etc.) that fits in your earring!

Never mind, neither of us has our ears pierced.

5:11 p.m.

We aren't getting anywhere. Taking a cheese break.

5:26 p.m.

Then Lada had an idea.

I think we should finish what we started.

What did we start?

The FUN research.

I felt kind of bad because technically I finished the fun research by myself when I asked Sunny to be on our team. Lada made the very good point that since she wasn't there to verify my findings, we probably should do it again together in a more scientifically controlled environment. I can't say I'm THAT excited about doing yet another scary thing, but from a scientific perspective, Lada is right. Plus, it'll probably be way less scary if we do it together.

What's an Earth fear you haven't conquered yet?

. . . .

BOUNCY HOUSES.

Bouncy-House Brainstorm

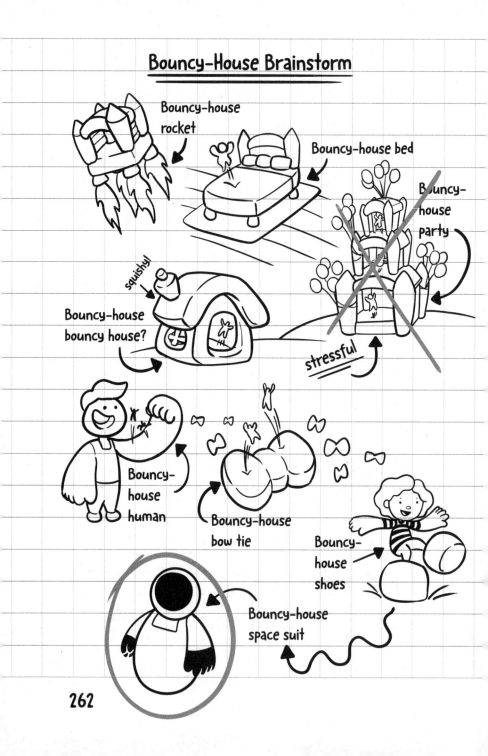

Bouncy-house rocket

Bouncy-house bed

Bouncy-house party

Bouncy-house bouncy house?

squishy!

stressful

Bouncy-house human

Bouncy-house bow tie

Bouncy-house shoes

Bouncy-house space suit

I stayed at Lada's ALL DAY on Saturday, and then we talked on the phone all day today. I'm pretty sure this bouncy-house suit idea is a winner.

Invention Convention Worksheet #1

Project Proposal: The Bouncy Suit ™

Team Members: Maple McNutt and Lada ~~Quiche Keesh~~ Kis

1.) Describe a problem in society that needs a solution:

One major problem in society that needs a solution is that, according to Bounce House Horror Stories, bouncy houses cause more injuries than shark attacks every year. Unfortunately, due to the fact that sharks can have up to 50 rows of razor-sharp teeth, and there is a whole week dedicated to them on TV, many people do not know the truth about bouncy houses until it's too late.

2.) How will your invention solve that problem?

Our invention will solve the problem by making a safe alternative to bouncy houses that keeps all the bounce without any of the death. We will do this by creating an inflatable bouncy suit so that you can bounce on the go, but safely.

Our proposal has officially been submitted! Lada and I have SO MUCH work to do. I told my mom that I probably wouldn't have time to empty the dishwasher this week, but she said I could find some time.

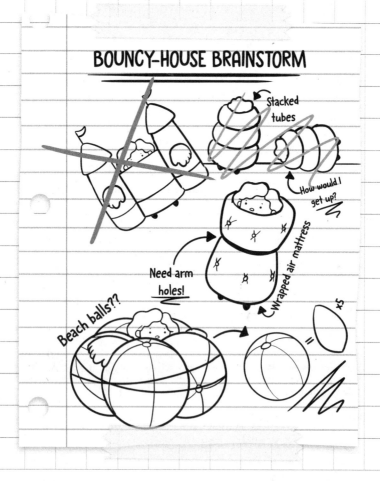

BOUNCY-HOUSE BRAINSTORM

Stacked tubes

How would I get up?

Wrapped air mattress

Need arm holes!

Beach balls??

x5

Lada came over to my house after school, and we went through my dad's miscellaneous room, a.k.a. the junk shed in the backyard. I warned her that his shed doesn't reflect my personal standards of organization, but she said she didn't mind at all.

You wouldn't believe the kinds of stuff we found in there.

THE JUNK SHED

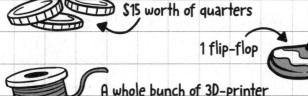

$15 worth of quarters

1 flip-flop

A whole bunch of 3D-printer plastic I didn't even know about!

My dad's old board games that were taking up too much space in the house

DO NOT TOUCH!

Some rusty tools that could give us a tetanus infection, so I told Lada to be careful

Juniper's camping gear that my mom said was too smelly to be in the house

2 dead cockroaches that Lada kindly removed

A deflated old air mattress

Lada and I took a brief break to wrap the air mattress around ourselves and pretend to be old ladies.

Back in the old country . . .

Back in my day . . .

Okay, back to work. We measured the air mattress and confirmed that we would have enough for two suits, plus a little extra in case Lada didn't cut within the lines.

Invention Convention Worksheet #2

Invention Name: __The Bouncy Suit ™__

Team Members: __Maple McNutt and Lada Kis__

1.) What materials will you need?

- Air mattress
- Thread
- Sewing needle (x 2)
- Inflation valve (x2)
- Glue

2.) Sketch your design.

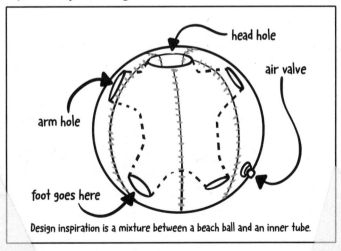

Design inspiration is a mixture between a beach ball and an inner tube.

267

Small problem: neither of us knows how to sew. Going to look up some tutorials on YouTube.

Lada and I are now experts on sewing. I finished four stitches already, which I know isn't THAT many, but I think they look pretty good:

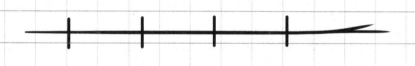

Lada already finished 400 stitches, but they look more like this:

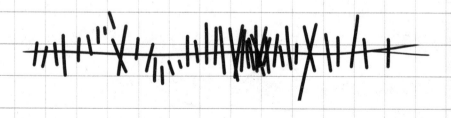

Between the two of us, I'm pretty sure it will at a minimum be really functional.

Invention Convention Worksheet #3

Invention Name: __The Bouncy Suit ™__

Team Members: __Maple McNutt and Lada Kis__

Construction Process:

1. Cut out all pieces of air mattress according to design.

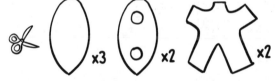

2. Sewed together all the pieces using a needle and thread.

These two pieces were not cut very neatly by one of the team members, and so we needed to recut them.

This part had a hole in it, so we applied a rhythmic gymnastics ribbon patch.

Lada is taller, so we had to make her suit 3.2 inches bigger. We also had to make a pocket for Lada's emergency cheese bunny storage.

269

3. Modeled an air inflation valve using Sculptibot3D with help from a beach ball purchased from Z-Mart.

4. 3D-printed the inflation valve in purple and black. It took 17.2 hours.

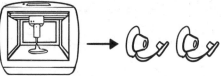

5. Poked a hole in the suits and glued the valve in place.

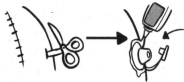

6. Trial inflation #1

    a. Failure. Air escaped through the seams. Reinforcing interior with a lot of duct tape.

7. Trial inflation #2

    a. Failure. Maple passed out while blowing into valve. She was resuscitated with vitamin water, cheese bunnies, and rest. Bike pump acquired.

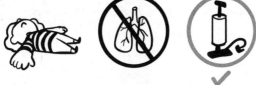

8. Trial inflation #3

    a. Success.

9. Applied bow tie for decoration.

I'm realizing that I've barely thought about Sunny at all since we got started on the Bouncy Suit. I guess I'm thinking about him right now, but that doesn't count. I'm so glad I don't have to do K-Rap ever again.

Recent Thoughts

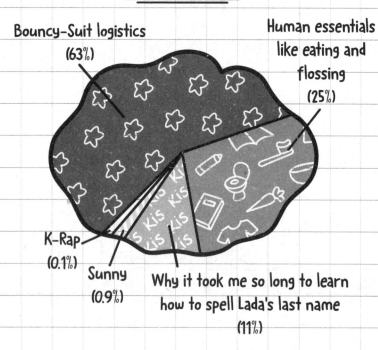

Bouncy-Suit logistics (63%)

Human essentials like eating and flossing (25%)

K-Rap (0.1%)

Sunny (0.9%)

Why it took me so long to learn how to spell Lada's last name (11%)

Invention Convention: Final Presentation

Invention Name: _The Bouncy Suit ™_

Team Members: _Maple McNutt and Lada Kis_

Only one week to go, folks! Prepare a five-minute presentation to showcase your invention to the judges at this Saturday's Invention Convention. Feel free to use additional props, visuals, or audience members to assist you. And don't forget to have fun!

> When: Saturday, 10:00 a.m.
> (Setup beginning at 9:00 a.m.)
> NASA Convention Center, Starship Gallery
> Bring your friends and family! Winner and prizes will be announced at noon.

Monday, 11:24 a.m.

I know that the actual inventing part is supposed to be the hardest, but it's the presentation I dread the most. Five minutes maybe doesn't SOUND like a lot, but just imagine: it's enough time to go into cardiac arrest, die for a WHOLE MINUTE, and then be completely revived.

Things that could go wrong:

1. My voice box gets paralyzed.

2. I bounce into a fork.

POP!

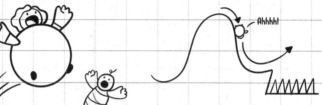

Ahhhh!

3. I bounce into a baby.

4. I roll down a hill, off a cliff, and onto a field of sharp spikes.

Just awful.

HELP!

5. The judges hate the suit.

6. I barf in the suit and drown in my own barf.

I suggested to Lada that maybe she should say all the words, and I would visually demonstrate the suit by standing next to her the whole time. We wouldn't even need to do any actual bouncing in public if Lada does a good job explaining the concept!

Lada unfortunately disagreed. She feels REALLY sure that we should trade off on the speaking part, and that we can hide note cards in our suits with the whole speech on them. She feels especially sure that at the end we should bounce together.

That sounds good in theory, but I've been in the world long enough to know that things never go according to plan.

4:49 p.m.

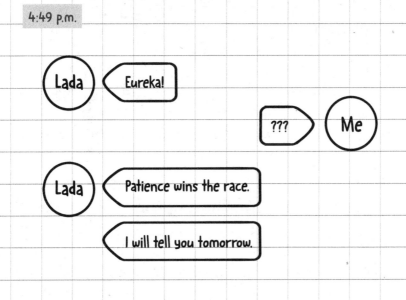

275

After computer science, Lada made me go to her
locker so she could give me something "really crucial."
She handed me the box from my "I'm Sorry, Lada"
Kit, although she'd repurposed it into an "Invention
Convention Survival Kit."

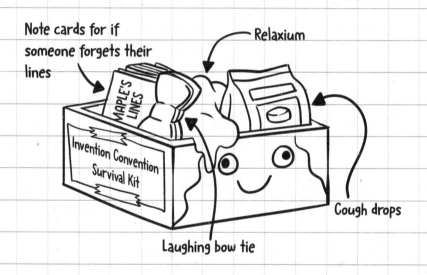

Note cards for if someone forgets their lines

Relaxium

Invention Convention Survival Kit

MAPLE'S LINES

Cough drops

Laughing bow tie

Lada explained that if anything went wrong during the
presentation, I could just use my kit. Then Lada told me
I needed to sit down so she could give me a pep talk.

Her pep talk made me miss the bus, so Uncle Belly dropped me off at home.

Lada might be the most thoughtful person I have ever met.

I went through the survival kit again and added a few things, like my backup BACKUP note cards. And my nebula Band-Aids. And my eco-straw just in case the NASA Space Center is under attack and we're stuck without clean water for days.

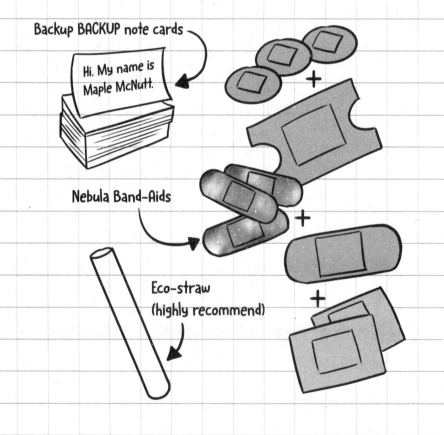

Backup BACKUP note cards

Hi. My name is Maple McNutt.

Nebula Band-Aids

Eco-straw (highly recommend)

Lada came over today to troubleshoot. We performed our presentation for my mom six times, and I wanted to do a seventh, but my mom said she needed to make sure we got Lada home so we could all go to bed.

PRESENTATION QUALITY CHECK

Run-Through 1	Okay. Lada forgot two lines.	✓−
Run-Through 2	Perfect	✓+
Run-Through 3	Pretty good. Maple coughed.	✓
Run-Through 4	Perfect	✓+
Run-Through 5	Perfect	✓+
Run-Through 6	Okay. Lada sneezed, had to blow nose, went overtime.	✓−
Run-Through 7	Aborted	✗

Friday, 11:37 a.m.

Lada made me change my alarm to "Heart of a Champion" so I could wake up before the convention tomorrow with the right mindset. We also did some mindful meditation on the track, which turned into me throwing cheese bunnies at Lada and seeing if she could catch them in her mouth.

Lada caught FOUR!

And I ALMOST caught ONE!

9:48 p.m.

Good night! Twelve more hours until we make history.

Waking up to "Heart of a Champion" really worked. I felt so pumped that when I ran into Juniper in the hallway, I gave her a double high five. Then I brushed my teeth with my hard-bristle toothbrush, because I knew I could take it today.

I was double skipping down the stairs when I heard the front door rattle, like maybe there was an invader trying to break into our home (and steal all my intellectual property right before the convention!). I ducked behind the kitchen wall to hide, but when the door opened, it wasn't a burglar at all. It was my dad!

Dad!

He had said he wasn't sure he'd be able to make it in time, but he just barely got the last flight out of California last night. I couldn't believe it! He even brought back a jar of my favorite apple butter!

While we all ate toast and apple butter in the kitchen, I showed my dad all the key diagrams in my journal to get him up to speed on our bouncy-house suit. I told him that since he was here, he could even help me inflate it!

7:58 a.m.

Now that I've gone to the bathroom three times, it's time to put my suit on. Getting the bouncy suit on is basically as complicated as an astronaut getting dressed for space. That's why I'm having BOTH my parents serve as my suit technicians. I asked Juniper to put my bow tie on for me, but she said I could do that myself.

282

Human stabilizer

air pump

Unfortunately, we didn't take car door sizes into account when designing the suit, so I had to deflate the suit to get into the car. I'll keep that in mind for the upgraded version. Maybe by that point, Over the Rainbowtie™ will have taken off and we can get my parents a special company car.

9:09 a.m.

When we got to NASA's Space Center, I immediately

spotted Lada in her bouncy suit waddling out of Uncle Belly's van.

Lada was there with Dr. Katarina and both her uncles. I told my dad that he should try to be smart around Dr. Katarina, since she is a highly acclaimed scientist at NASA and her daughter is my BEST friend. My dad said, "I'll try."

Luckily, Dr. Katarina was really friendly and didn't say anything too complicated. I think my mom even made Dr. Katarina laugh! I'll have to keep my eye on them since it would be in the interest of my and Lada's future research for our families to get along.

9:16 a.m.

The Invention Convention is taking place in the Starship Gallery at NASA, which is my second-favorite gallery after the Astronaut Gallery. There are all kinds of

moon-rock samples just sitting out, and an ACTUAL
Apollo spacecraft! I reminded Lada as we came inside
that we were making history.

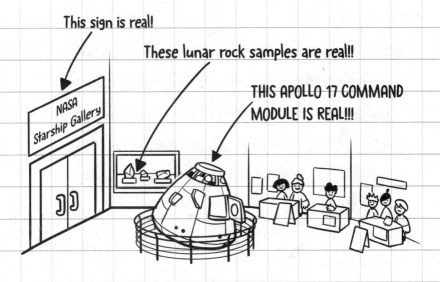

This sign is real!

These lunar rock samples are real!!

THIS APOLLO 17 COMMAND
MODULE IS REAL!!!

NASA
Starship Gallery

Mr. Wormley told us that we were free to go around
the room to look at all the other projects with our
families. Only 44 minutes until judging begins!

We directed Lada's uncles so they could help us lay
out important demonstration materials; then Lada
filled in as my suit technician and reinflated my suit.

285

Dr. Katarina took a picture of us, but I asked her to retake it since Lada didn't have her bow tie on yet. Dr. Katarina said, "You got it, scientists!"

I'm not going to lie, it's been a little difficult writing in this journal while wearing my bouncy suit. But if I pause every few minutes and curl up into a ball inside my suit, then I can balance the journal on my knee. I just have to be really careful not to pop the air mattress with my pencil.

9:42 a.m.

I feel like the Timber Cove STEM sixth-grade class really brought their A game this year.

Lars Ip and Kelvin Juma invented Drool$_2$O, a machine that recycles drool from your pillow into drinking water. Dr. Katarina was really impressed, although she politely declined when Lars offered her a cup.

Libby Bimburg, Trudy Su, and Chester Bog came up with shoes called LifeFupps, which are just those expensive Fupp shoes except they can also inflate into floaties in case of a flash flood.

Stayla Shi invented a board game that's a horse murder mystery where you have to figure out who killed "Stranger, the black stallion." My dad was very interested in the gameplay.

Horse card

WHO KILLED STRANGER?

START

Avenge me!

Justice!

Ovi Nagar showed off the Hair-Hairbrush, which he said was "the brush by your hair, for your hair." My mom asked him what that meant, and he explained that he had been growing a rattail for seven years and finally cut it off to use it in the brush. My mom did not ask any more questions.

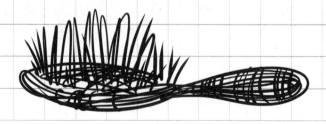

Lada feels pretty confident that we're going to win, and I think I agree.

9:54 a.m.

Well, Lada and I aren't feeling quite as confident after seeing Mahogany Perez's invention. I don't know how she did it, but she made an app called "Do You Like Me?" that uses facial recognition to tell if someone likes you. We thought it was GROUNDBREAKING, although Mahogany was bummed that when she pointed the app at Lars Ip, it said he didn't like her. Dr. Katarina was VERY impressed and said NASA could use a mind like hers one day. NASA is a pretty big place, so there's almost definitely room for both of us.

♥ Do You Like Me?
Look at the camera and
LET'S FIND OUT!

We were heading back to our booth when we heard shouting coming from two rows down. Lada and I waddled over and saw Sunny making an announcement in front of the K-Rap booth. I'm pretty sure we made eye contact for a second, but then he quickly looked away.

Ladiiiesss and gentlemen and gentlehumans! Special demonstration of the greatest K-Rap routine EVERRRR in exactly one minute!!!

That turned out to be a misleading statement. Jared spent about two minutes yelling at Sunny for forgetting the hair gel and then yelling at his mom for not pointing the light in the right spot.

290

When they started actually performing, Lada was NOT impressed. She said they should rename it OK-Rap because it's only okay. I told her it was worse than OK-Rap—it was . . . you know. She didn't know, so I whispered it.

krap.

Lada laughed so hard, I thought she might pop her suit, so we left to go get ready for our demonstration. Also, I'm pretty sure they're going to throw Sunny into the air at the end, and that makes me nervous.

10:15 a.m.

Mr. Wormley got on the stage and said the judging was going to start in 10 minutes. And apparently, they have a "truly spectacular" lineup for us. The first judge will be none other than Mr. Wormley, followed by Ms. Staples from the computer science department. And last, we have a very special guest judge—the one, the only

Oh. My. GOSH.

JACKIE GRAND.

Are you getting this? Jackie Grand is HERE in the building, as we speak! I turned to Lada and asked if she heard Mr. Wormley's announcement, and she said yes. So I'm probably not unconscious and just dreaming the whole thing.

I feel like maybe my ankylosing spondylitis is returning and paralyzing my voice box, so Lada should probably do the demo by herself.

10:18 a.m.

Lada just reminded me that she packed the Invention

292

Convention Survival Kit for this very reason. I got out my Relaxium and took five deep breaths.

10:21 a.m.

The Relaxium is not really helping. Jackie Grand is currently <50 feet away from our booth, and it's looking like my condition is permanent. I told Lada that I don't want to ruin her chances of getting a minor planet named after her, so I should quit ASAP. She gave me her Relaxium and suggested I try the double squish.

Relaxium

Oh gosh, I can't feel my feet or my face or really any part in between.

=Numb

Remember that my ashes are supposed to be sprinkled in space. I leave my bouncy suit to Lada. Don't worry about giving Sunny his geode back.

Jackie is exactly FOUR BOOTHS AWAY.

Lada, the chances that I'll even be able to say "hi" are less than 1%.

What if we reprogram the bow tie to say "Hi, Jackie Grand?"

That was a good idea, so we recorded me saying it, and even though it was wobbly, you could at least understand it.

10:35 a.m.

Jackie Grand is one booth away. Lada gave me a
cough drop.

10:39 a.m.

The judges are coming! It's time!

10:58 a.m.

UPDATE: A LOT HAPPENED.

Lada said, "Greetings, esteemed judges," and then it
was my turn, but I couldn't say anything (of course),
so I pressed the bow tie as planned. I guess we didn't
reprogram it properly, because instead of saying "Hi,
Jackie Grand," it played the track of Lada's family
laughing really hard.

Everything went quiet for a second, but then all
three judges laughed, INCLUDING JACKIE! She asked

296

about my bow tie, and I explained that it was
actually an old invention Lada and I had developed to
generate humor. And once I started talking, I sort of
couldn't stop?

> So Lada and I had this whole project to figure out how
> to be fun, and we came up with 4 CRUCIAL elements.

> We invented lots of things WAY BEFORE the Invention
> Convention EVEN STARTED for the first three elements.

> The Bouncy Suit is our fourth and
> final element, which is to do
> something scary!

> It's the cherry on top
> of the ice cream
> sundae of science!!

I even started telling her about the time I couldn't
get on the bouncy-house obstacle course and it

actually caused me to miss out on getting her autograph, but then Mr. Wormley told me I was in danger of going over my five-minute presentation time. Lada gave me a double thumbs-up, and we decided to move into the bouncing portion of our presentation.

It went pretty much PERFECTLY.

We bounced into various objects, including the wall, my mom, and each other. We also demonstrated the earthquake mode, where Lada dropped every book in the Apothecary's Daughter series onto me, but I came out completely unharmed! We also demonstrated spaceflight mode, where I sat in a chair in my suit and Lada shook the chair really hard but I was completely protected. I told Jackie that I really want to be an astronaut one day and that the suit could be a useful addition to astronaut training protocols.

The judges must have been really impressed, because they clapped so loudly that I could hear it from inside the suit.

Jackie said that she agreed with me and could see the suit "assisting with atmospheric reentry training." Mr. Wormley said he applauded our personal connection to the invention. Ms. Staples said she liked the bow ties.

As the judges started making their way to the next booth, Lada pointed to my notebook and said, "Ask her!" I was confused for a second, but then I knew what Lada was talking about.

And then this happened:

Wait for it. . . .

Wait for it. . . .

SEE YOU AT NASA!!
— JACKIE GRAND

I told Lada that I needed a moment to process my feelings, so that's why I'm sitting by myself on the floor next to the water fountain. I should probably go soon, because I've been here for thirteen minutes, and Lars Ip is emptying out all his drool water.

11:22 a.m.

Lada and I are going to get a snack to celebrate. I can't believe I actually spoke entire words to Jackie Grand!

11:36 a.m.

I wonder if Jackie will remember this day forever as well!

11:43 a.m.

My mom and Dr. Katarina wanted to take more pictures of us in the suits, so we said sure. I meant to say "cheese" but I accidentally said "Jackie Grand."

Uncle Danish is not great at personal space.

11:50 a.m.

The judges left to deliberate. Lada said she was a little nervous about the results, so I gave back her Relaxium and also my Relaxium so she could try the double squish.

11:58 a.m.

They're about to announce the winners! Lada is squeezing my hand (and the Relaxium) really hard.

Mr. Wormley said that this year we had a lot of really great inventions, and choosing just three winners was one of the hardest things he's ever had to do. Jackie Grand nodded her head in agreement, although I'm 99.9% sure she's had to do way harder things.

Third place goes to . . . Lars Ip and Kelvin Juma for the Drool$_2$O!

Second place goes to . . . US!!!!!

Lada screamed so loud that I jumped. Luckily, I was still in the bouncy suit, so I'm okay. Lada and I tried to hug, but it's really hard to execute a clean hug in the bouncy suits so we did more of a chest bump.

First place went to Mahogany Perez!

We went onstage to accept our prizes. Lars and Kelvin each got a Timber Cove Middle School visor.

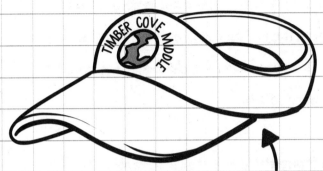

I felt a little bad, because we all already got these hats for Field Day.

Lada and I each got a $25 gift certificate to Scoopy's Ice Cream, which is basically the best ice cream shop within a fifteen-mile radius. And they sell real ice cream, none of that fake astronaut stuff.

Mahogany Perez got to choose the name of her minor planet. She said she wanted to name it Planet Lars, but Mr. Wormley said they could talk about that later.

12:28 p.m.

Lada and I decided that we should go out to ice cream
RIGHT NOW. I think my dad was starting to fall asleep a
little from jet lag, but he seemed to really perk up at
the idea of getting a "sundae with those little rainbow
morsels." I'll probably get mint chocolate chip, since it's
Jackie's favorite flavor.

My mom thought that it was pretty cool that Jackie
Grand was here. She said that somebody's parent
must've pulled some strings at NASA to organize that.
Then she elbowed me and said:

Maybe somebody in NASA's PR department, huh?

Basically everyone's parents work at NASA, so we'll probably never know.

Sunny came over just as we were leaving. He said
that our suits were reaaaallly cool and congrats
on second place. Lada said, "Can we help you?" and
hairy-eyeballed so hard at Sunny that I thought she
might pull an eyelid muscle.

Sunny mumbled some stuff about "that practice that
one time" and how "things didn't go as planned, you
know." Then Jared shouted from behind for Sunny to
come onnnnnn, they were going to get smoothies.

I'm pretty sure Sunny was trying to say sorry. I guess
I can stop being mad at him, although that doesn't

change my feelings about never wanting to participate in KRAP—I mean, K-Rap—ever again.

1:09 p.m.

Lada and I each got a mint chocolate chip ice cream sundae with a cherry on top. Victory tastes good, but I have to say, ice cream tastes WAY better. Or maybe they're tied? Inconclusive.

We sat at a separate table from the adults so we could discuss our fun research confidentially. We decided that the only thing left to do in a scientific report is to write a conclusion. So here goes:

Conclusion

Was the hypothesis correct?
Yes. Based on the data, we are now 100% fun. Well,
99.9% because 100% is nearly impossible in science.

Did you encounter any unexpected challenges?
Yes. We think there may be a side effect of becoming
fun, where you make bad decisions and lose sight of
your true friends. But fortunately, it's not permanent.

What advice would you have for other scientists who
are trying to prove their own theories?
Find a REALLY GOOD ~~research assistant.~~ ~~partner.~~ friend.

Lada spilled a little
ice cream.

You never know what the future may hold!

More sleepovers!

Ice cream!

Rhythmic gymnastics routine together?

I'll try!

More cheese boards!

Boards MADE of cheese!

More research experiments!

YES, PLEASE!

ACKNOWLEDGMENTS

To our agent, Alex Weiss, for taking this tiny seed of an idea and helping us transform it into a full-fledged human story. To our editor, Jessi Smith, for understanding this book so completely and shepherding it into the world. Thank you for bringing both the HAHAs and the heart. To Tiara Iandiorio, for making sure all the artwork—we mean, scientific diagrams—look their best. To Chel Morgan, who oversaw this project better than a flight director in mission control. To Karen Sherman, Stacey Sakal, and Bara MacNeill, who reviewed our manuscript with a level of precision we'd never witnessed before. To Emily McMillan, for helping us stay EXTREMELY true to Maple's voice. To Ankita Panda and Michael Lucchi, for the super scientific space consultations. To Kyle Gee, for double-checking our code (irzyt 4hk). To Nancy McMillan, for the hand-painted butterflies. (Did you know they use their feet to taste?!) To our parents, for supporting all our artistic experiments, no matter how messy or noisy they were.

ABOUT THE AUTHORS

KATE MCMILLAN grew up in Houston, Texas, illustrating and writing stories in the world's tiniest font. She studied architecture in college and received a fellowship to research traditional boatbuilding in Norway. She has worked as a concept artist for animation studios, including Disney and DreamWorks. In her free time, she enjoys building furniture and drawing wobbly buildings that look like they might fall down.

RUTHIE PRILLAMAN is a writer and musician from Potomac, Maryland. She received her BA in English literature and her MFA in screenwriting. Her creative career has spanned writing for television, creating classical music for kids, and playing in an electro-folk band with her brother. Outside of work, she enjoys singing in choirs and cooking Hungarian goulash in her traditional goulash pot.

31901070136256